ABSAROKA VALLEY

ABSAROKA VALLEY

LAURAN PAINE

BLACK STONE PUBLISHING

Printed in the United States of America

ISBN 978-1-982594-92-3
Fiction / Westerns

1 3 5 7 9 10 8 6 4 2

CIP data for this book is available
from the Library of Congress

Blackstone Publishing
31 Mistletoe Rd.
Ashland, OR 97520

www.BlackstonePublishing.com

CHAPTER ONE

The man stood watching dawn break, like a creeping wraith, into the black whispering mass of trees where his wagon stood. There was a ground fog, watery white and clinging, to this new day; it gently ebbed and it gently flowed. The sun would come as it always did and burn this shroud from earth, but meanwhile, there it was, dirty white and diluted looking, weak and watery and yet in its own way strong enough to be choking and suffocating and evil.

He moved to poke at the little fire near his feet which outlined his lankness with its flickering light, his cracked old boots and his wasted face. Then he turned slightly to gaze upon two little lumps upon the nearby ground, curled deep in soiled quilts and old ragged blankets. These were his children, Linda Louise, eight years of age, and Billy Ray, ten.

Yonder stood the patient mules, old and scarred and wise as

only aged animals can be wise. Their harness hung upon the wagon tongue, along with two dented buckets and a settler's axe and spade.

That white mist swirled into the first fringe of red-barked pines; it came creeping through dawn's utter stillness. The lank man pushed fisted big hands into pockets to watch its coming. But it never got to the wagon, the gaunt big man, or to the busy little fire, for that widening great stain of light over the eastern hills turned from pink to brightest gold, and the sun came, popped up from behind those hills like a seed is popped from a grape.

It was a summertime sun, all dancing gold and swollen, and its cauldron-like heat rushed down over the land in blinding waves to jump into canyons, to flash up along mountainsides, to burn with merciless intensity into that miasmic flow of dirty white. It cut in among the trees to warm the backs of those standing mules, to lay a shaded pattern across the gaunt man's wasted face, to brighten the undersides of two pairs of closed eyelids and awaken Linda Louise and Billy Ray Patton.

Their father watched how his children simply looked up and smiled at him, ready in that single, uncomplicated instant, to arise and move and run to the creek to wash, to happily chatter, and he thought what a blessed thing youth was; how blind and trusting and utterly unquenchable it was. He smiled back at them and hunkered low by the fire to put on the pot of mush, mixed with the last of that milk they'd acquired miles back at a village. He stirred this weak porridge and indifferently considered their onward passage down the land upon the golden carpet of a fresh new day.

He heard them at the creek, squealing at the coldness of that water, and his heart was heavy for them, and it was also weary from its tired and sluggish beating, for it knew there was no hope; that he would tool his wagon endlessly onward seeking something which did not exist upon this earth—surcease, peace, safety for his children. A man in his yeasty years stepped over the tallest mountains, paced the widest plains, braved the brawlingest rivers in search of a mate.

Samuel Patton had done these things; he had found her in a Mormon settlement beyond the big Missouri. He had taken frail Kathleen Bryan to be his wife, and his heart had been full to overflowing, for Kathleen had dark and misty eyes and a dreamy way to her. She had been soft and eager for his touch. She had borne him Billy Ray with his mother's gentleness and his father's pale blue eyes. She had borne him Linda Louise with her mother's liquid dark eyes and taffy hair. And Kathleen had died in the mud beside the Osage River after a six weeks' deluge of steady drizzle, dead at twenty-one of lung fever.

Samuel had nursed her. For all his bigness in those days, his mighty strength and his power, he had been as tender with Kathleen as with a new lamb. He had never left her side. But she had died, and he buried her in the mud bottoms where fragile willows grew, and he had then hitched up and gone on.

That had been some years back. Time had, after a while, healed his hurt, but a kind of exhaustion had come to Samuel. With it had come this wasting. The year before, a doctor in a Rocky Mountain settlement had told him: "Sir, it is not the memory which makes you weary in body. Sir, you have lung fever."

He stirred that weak porridge.

There was no cure that the doctors knew of; a man lost his strength a little at a time, his flesh wasted, he awoke in the mornings tired, and he felt within him the diminishing of his proud spirit.

But a man never drew in a vital big gust of good fresh air in his lifetime, Samuel Patton knew, without also drawing in, each day, a little of the decay of death also, for this was the sum of a man's existence. No matter who he was, how great or small, how mighty or how weak, each morning he was one more new day closer to eternity. It was not, therefore, the gift of life Samuel was loath to put aside; it was his children which made the hopelessness in his breast so bitter. They had no other kin, and in this savage frontier land, each family had a cleaving only for its own. Life here was hard, food and safety were dearly wrung from the soil, and aimlessly wandering strangers could count on sympathy only, which was never enough, because sympathy was a variety of deceit. It was another way for people to feel secretly glad the troubles of others had happened to strangers and not themselves.

Still, as long as life lasted, men struggled. In the Bible it said man was born to strife, to suffering, to anguish. So long, then, as life lasted, Samuel Patton must continue his search. This was his private struggle. Find a place for his children somewhere in this savage land. Find love and a cherishing appreciation for these two precious gifts Kathleen had left him. Until he found these things, he must keep going, must ignore as best he could that insidiously creeping thralldom which bowed down his spirit and mightily taxed his waning strength, for no man lacks a goal, not even a wasting man burdened with lung fever who saw in the morning mist the solitude and peacefulness of death, against which he had, each new day, to summon all his remaining strength to stave off for yet a while, what was inevitable.

"Pa," said a solemn little voice behind him. "Pa, there's a man and a big black horse down by the creek."

Samuel turned. Linda Louise was there, her face pink from cold water, her flawless dark eyes big and round and very solemn.

"Well," answered Samuel, "invite him along for some porridge made from milk."

"We can't, Pa. Billy Ray is down there with him. We can't get him up."

Samuel considered his daughter. She was small for her age but sturdy. She would, one day, be a beautiful woman, as her mother had also been. Her face was alive to life, shadows of passing moods altered it constantly. She was, in Samuel's eyes, more nearly the pure mixture of himself and his Kathleen than was their son Billy Ray, and now, studying her gravity, feeling her mild puzzlement, Samuel sensed the quiet awe which held his little girl there motionless and waiting, as though in her perplexity, she had come to the only person on earth in whom she reposed fullest trust, full confidence.

She had not a single doubt but that her father would be able to explain about the man and the big black horse down by the creek. So she stood still, waiting.

Samuel gravely arose. He took her hand and went along with her where trees thinned out, where a grassy glade spread up and down a fluting-swift run of good snow water. There, Linda Louise led him northward. There, he found his son squatting in shade, solemnly gazing upon a saddled black horse whose head hung low and whose flanks were close tucked from fatigue and foodlessness.

"There, Pa," said Linda Louise, releasing Samuel's hand, putting both arms behind her to stand back a ways looking down into the grass. "That's him. Is he asleep?"

Samuel knew at once this man was not asleep. Wariness came up in him. He went forward very carefully, then stood gazing upon that sprawled, still form. There was a faint fluttering rise and fall to the stranger's chest. He was a tall man, as tall as Samuel himself was. He was well-dressed in dark clothing and the shell belt encircling his narrow waist sagged from the weight of a large black gun.

Samuel had a feeling about this man. He turned to see the horse. A carbine butt stuck upright, ready to hand on the saddle's right side. There was a tightly bound bedroll aft of the cantle and there were engraved silver ornaments upon the saddle, the headstall, and the bit.

From upon the ground, Samuel's son said: "Pa, did you ever see such a fine horse? There's no white on him anywhere."

Samuel looked away from the animal, back down to the man.

He knelt, rolled that inert form over upon its back, and saw at once where the bullet had struck low along the stranger's right side, angling upward as though the injured man had been riding and the man who had shot him had been upon the ground.

"Linda Louise, I'll need a pan of water," Samuel said. "Fetch one of the clean towels too, honey. They are under the chuck box in the back of the wagon."

Linda Louise hastened away. Billy Ray left off admiring the black horse and came over to stare down past his father's shoulder as Samuel cleanly cut away that blood-stiff shirt.

"Golly," said Billy Ray, in awe. "He's bad hurt, isn't he, Pa?"

"Yes. But he'll likely live."

There were three broken ribs, and the stranger's flesh was torn ragged and swollen badly. It was purple for the long length of his injury.

"Did his horse throw him, Pa? Maybe he landed on a boulder, or a snag limb, to get torn up like that, huh?"

Samuel had never been a good man to compromise with truth. He said: "We'll have to get him to the wagon, son." He did not answer Billy Ray's question at all. "Maybe the three of us could drag him there."

Billy Ray said logically: "His horse could carry him, Pa."

Samuel looked up. He smiled at his son's good sense.

"You're plumb right, boy. But first we've got to fix this hurt."

Linda Louise returned with towels and water from the creek. She and her brother helped Samuel bandage the stranger. They also helped him boost the man to his feet, get him across the black horse's back, and slowly lead the laden animal to their wagon. There, they made the injured stranger comfortable upon a bed of their quilts, covered him, and turned next to breaking their camp.

It was Billy Ray's responsibility to catch and harness their mules.

Linda Louise ran to the creek with the breakfast pans, scoured them with silt, and ran back to put everything into its allotted place. Samuel, deep in troubled thought, ate his porridge slowly. He was the last to be ready when the children had their chores finished. They had gulped down their breakfast in the manner of excited little animals long before, each with a special reason. Linda Louise wished to nurse the stranger. Billy Ray had in mind riding the big black horse behind the wagon when they moved out.

Samuel finally arose, went along the wagon's side as was his custom at each camp-breaking, seeing that the axe, the shovel, the pots and pans were all put away, that the chain-tugs had been properly hooked, the chocks removed from under the wagon's wheels, and nothing had been forgotten. Those tasks completed, he went up hand-over-hand to the high seat, peered down inside the wagon at his daughter where she solemnly sat curled by the unconscious stranger, then around where Billy Ray sat proudly upon the stranger's black horse, and flipped the lines.

Beyond their camp, beyond the final last fringe of forest, lay a long valley. Distantly, there were bony mountain flanks squatting low, pinching that long valley down to a narrow, funnel-like yonder outlet. Samuel imagined how the road would be through that pass—rocky and bumpy but passable. He had passed through a hundred passes just like that. And somewhere on ahead would be a town or a village, or perhaps only a hamlet.

Sunlight burned its steady scald over the land, but the real heat would not come for another two hours—it was still early in this day. For a time they would all feel good. Their bellies were full, their attentions were occupied, and around them was the swollen richness of nature's greenery, her trees and grasses and upland flowers.

Samuel twisted now and then for a rearward look. Billy Ray sat the black horse, now with a smile, now with a scowl; he alternated between the sweet delight of youth and the splendid imaginings of himself as a great scout, or mighty general, or of a knight in finely etched armor.

Under the wagon bows, in shade made of the canvas top, Linda Louise sat on with her patient, from time to time putting cool rags soaked in the water barrel across his sweating forehead. The stranger himself bumped limply along. His face steadily reddening from fever, his lips hot and cracking. He opened his eyes occasionally, Samuel noticed, but there was no focus, no rationalization at all, to this misty staring.

Where the valley drew out thin, where the mountains began to tilt inward and downward, Samuel found the old argonaut trail exactly as he had known he would. It showed clearly that little traffic had passed over it in years, but his old mules were wise; they knew how to step around boulders, to sidle clear of stones large enough to hang the wagon upon high-centering obstacles. They made the transition from valley to mountain pass without difficulty, and where this downward trail fell away abruptly, they knew how to ride back on their breechings so that the wagon did not creep up and nudge them.

This old road hugged granite cliffs in a long-spending curve leading steadily downward to an immense plain. From his place upon the high seat, Samuel looked far out and down.

This land they were approaching was cattle country. One did not have to see the actual cattle to know. One had only to have been a husbandman once himself to know.

A summertime haze hung above that immense prairie. Lower, where this smokiness writhed under the steady buildup of relentless heat, there was a long winding creek bed willow-shaded and passing on out of sight southward.

Still farther out, dimly unreal appearing, stood a giant sawtoothed mountain range, and even from this distance, Samuel

could plainly see where sunlight flashed pale pink upon the snow
fields, high up there.

It took two hours to make that cautious and perilous ascent,
but once the prairie floor was reached, Samuel paused to rest his
mules. Here, close to the base of the foothill, there remained a
lingering night-like coolness. Here too, coming straight out of solid
granite, was the pouring freshet which fed that southward creek
bed lined with willows.

Samuel thought of finishing the day here. There was rich good
grass, shade, and solitude. But he did not. He pushed onward again,
out across the prairie, and kept traveling all that afternoon until
red sunlight warned him of day's end. Then, seven miles clear of
those rearward mountains, he halted in a greenery thicket, drove
the wagon out of sight here, and made his camp. Afterward, with
the children going happily about their chores, Samuel walked back
a ways to stand in the dying light, watching their back trail. There
was nothing to see. The land lay still and quiet and entirely empty.

He went back to the little stone ring Billy Ray had built, knelt
there in silence, and began coaxing a cooking fire to life. Linda
Louise made a little squeal from the creek, and immediately afterward Billy Ray's laughter came kiting over the splash of water.

Samuel set up his pot tripod and put the remainder of their
breakfast mush to heating. He also set a pan of water to boil, and
afterward, he looked out where the stranger's black horse was
contentedly browsing with the mules, then closer, where Billy
Ray had dumped the stranger's expensive saddle and bridle. He
considered that saddle for a long time, seeing its saddlebags, its
canteen, and bedroll. He rose up, passed over to these things,
bent low to flip back the saddlebag straps, and reach inside.

He stiffened his full length, staring down at what he'd partially
revealed in one withdrawn hand—a crushed packet of crisp green
money!

CHAPTER TWO

They trailed downland the next day, starting early, as Samuel said, to avoid some of the day's heat, and they nooned in more willows then kept to their southward way.

In a wagon one could only make good traveling time by steadily moving onward. They could not speed along as mounted people might. Samuel kept moving. He did not know exactly why he was doing this. He did know that somewhere far back, men were rummaging the land with guns for his weak and wounded passenger. He wished for the stranger not to be caught. But why he wished this, he could not have precisely explained.

Samuel Patton had always been an honest man. He had come upon outlaws at other times, and he had been stoutly opposed to all they stood for. He was perplexed in his spirit now, thinking over his actions. It was a solid conviction in his mind that the feverishly moaning man in his wagon was an outlaw. He rode too fine a horse for an ordinary man. He wore a gun as only a man wears weapons who lives by them. And of course that saddlebag full of paper money was in its own mute way a testimony of evil.

Still, the stranger was a man, and because of this he deserved at least an even chance. In his present semiconscious condition, he would stand no chance at all if overtaken by pursuers whose anger and vengeance found him hurt and helpless.

Samuel kept to his steady southward course, prudent enough to stay always within the obscuring shadows of that willow-lined creek. He knew that a pursuing posse coming out far back upon those granite headlands could look outward and downward upon this vast plain and instantly sight movement—unless that movement was hidden by screening shade. A man did not survive childhood and come to manhood on the frontier without learning a few basic rules for continued existence. Samuel was such a man. Once, in fact, he had been more than simply prudent. But that had been years back.

* * * * *

The second day, while they were breaking camp at dawn with those highland snowfields and their containing great mountains close bulking, large, and dark against a paling sky, Linda Louise came from feeding their passenger to where Samuel stood, saying: "Pa, Mr. Black wants to talk to you."

Samuel smiled. His children had named the man for his animal. The horse was called simply Big Black, and his owner was called Mr. Black.

"How is he?" asked Samuel of his daughter. "Did he eat?"

"Yes," Linda Louise reported. "He even asked about coffee. I told him we had none. Then he sat up and asked to talk to you, Pa."

"Well," said Samuel, "if he's beginning to want things, he must be much better." He started along for the wagon saying: "Tell Billy Ray to hold off harnessing up just yet."

Samuel drew aside the puckered rear canvas at the wagon's tailgate. He looked in where gloom lay thick and where their passenger was fingering a bristly growth of beard stubble. The man's face was sallow now, after the breaking of his fever. His lips were peeling, and his smoky gray eyes lay deep in their sockets.

Samuel said: "I'm glad to see you've come around, friend. It's been a hard haul for you."

He noticed that someone had brought the stranger's saddlebags to him; that they lay under the stranger's protective left hand and also that his six-gun lay in his lap. He met this man's unwavering gaze with an amiable look, waiting out the silence which dwelt between them.

The stranger licked his lips. He said, in a deep-toned way: "I'm obliged to you for what you've done. Your little girl told me how you found me . . . how you fixed me up and brought me along. I want to pay you for all that . . . It's the least I can do."

"We can talk of that later," replied Samuel. "We're fixing to break camp now. You rest, and maybe tonight, if you're up to it, we can visit a little."

The stranger considered this. He also considered the threadbare garments Samuel wore and how his big-boned frame stood out starkly under them at shoulder point, at breastbone, at wrist, and hip. He said softly: "All right. By the way, I'm called Jess." Samuel nodded at this, saying his own name and pushing out a hand. They shook, exchanging a long look, then Samuel moved clear, drew the canvas closed, and paced alongside the wagon, brows rolled inward a little pensively.

"Pa . . .?"

He turned. Billy Ray was there, holding the reins of the stranger's black horse.

"Does he want to ride his horse, or can I?"

"You can, son. His name is Jess, and he won't be up to riding for a few days yet."

Samuel looked around. Linda Louise was clambering over the tailgate. A sinewy arm went forth to help her. Billy Ray was going up the side of the black horse. Nothing lay forgotten at the campsite. Samuel stepped upon a wheel hub, caught the seat, and pulled himself up. He kicked off the brake, took up the lines, and said softly: "Jack. Jenny." And the wagon started forward.

The morning advanced, bringing on its heat haze to soften those onward bleak mountainsides. Samuel, no longer feeling the need for creek-side protection, drove out upon solider ground, keeping his steady gaze upon the lower down lifts and rises for some idea as to where he might find the pass which surely lay dead ahead out and over those mountains.

Sunlight eventually burned against the earth, sparkling with bitter little flashes from mica particles in the stony soil. It rolled solidly back from those mountainsides layer upon layer of it. The mules stirred this heat as they passed through it, sides glistening, legs mechanically moving, heads low and drowsily fixed ahead.

Samuel sweated. Such heat unnerved him, made him loose and bone-tired even without moving in it. Dust rose lazily to coat his throat and sting his eyes. He swung back to the shade of the willows again, and here the scent of water was good in an otherwise acrid atmosphere.

He came at long last to a place where venturing beavers from the nearby forested foothills had made a dam. There was a fine glassy pool of water behind this mud-and-twig obstruction. There was also shade and good grass. It was not yet late afternoon, but Samuel thought it was late enough, so he drew the wagon up close and halted it. Here, they would make their night camp.

Billy Ray at once cared for the big black horse. He afterward tended the mules and busily formed the stone ring for their supper fire. Linda Louise ran to that still water pool and stood there, delighted by it.

Samuel got down to go back and lower the tailgate, which served as supper table and work area. When he arrived there, he found Jess standing clear of the wagon in a fresh shirt, his gun strapped to him, staring far back with a solemn expression.

"You got no call to be up and around yet," said Samuel. "You need rest."

"A man gets restless," said Jess, turning back toward the tailgate, watching Samuel work the hasps. "I watched your boy today. He likes horses, doesn't he?"

"Like all boys do," murmured Samuel, working over their supper. "I don't think he's been fifty feet from that black horse of yours since we found you." Samuel swung his head, and he smiled. "They call him Big Black, and they named you Mr. Black, after him."

This brought up an answering smile. "It's as good a name as any," said Jess, and he looked steadily at the little pile of provisions the chuck box held. "There's a town through those mountains. I expect we'd better stock up when we get there."

Silently, Samuel worked on. After a while he said: "Do you know the pass through these mountains?"

"I know it all right," responded Jess. "I ought to anyway. I came up through here two months ago."

Samuel said nothing. He had the last of their salt pork sliced, ready for the frying. He turned toward the fire.

Behind him, Jess put a puzzled gaze upon Samuel, stood there silent and motionless for a long time. Then he went along to the fire, also, and eased down upon the ground.

"Linda Louise talked to me today," he said quietly.

"She likes company. She's only eight years old."

Samuel worked sluggishly but knowingly at his chore. He did not once look around at the man beside him.

"She told me lots of things . . . about her mother and about you. About the days and nights on the road. About Billy Ray, too."

"I guessed she would," said Samuel. "It's hard for a little girl . . . and a little boy . . . going on and on like this."

Jess let this go past without comment. He was watching Samuel closely now. "She told me something else, too. I reckon, when a man has troubles, he sometimes talks in his sleep."

Now Samuel turned his head. He had never told the children of his lung fever. Until this moment he had never thought they knew. Now, the premonition rose up solidly in him. "Yes," he said softly, "what did she tell you?"

"How her mother died. How you have the same ailment."

"I see. And she heard that from me in my sleep?"

"She did."

"Did she say Billy Ray knows too?"

"She said they both know, Samuel."

"Well!" exclaimed Samuel. Then more softly, thoughtfully: "Well." He lowered his head over the fry pan, turning that cooking meat with a Bowie knife, saying nothing more for a long time. Not until the meat was ready and the sun was dropping redly away in the smoky west.

"They would have learnt it all sooner or later. I had hoped it might be later, because there is yet much for me to do." Samuel lifted his head, swung it creekward, and kept it that way, as though listening for his children down at the glassy pool. "It doesn't matter who we are, does it?" he said. "Life hammers us all toward a common denominator. I have my problems, and you have yours."

Jess said: "I read something once . . . 'In a thorn thicket is the scent of tomorrow's unborn roses.'"

Samuel looked around at this tall, leaned-down stranger. Kept his gaze upon him for a long time. *That*, he thought, *is an odd thing for a renegade to say.* "If you'll hand me those tins, I'll dish up supper," he muttered, and took the plates without addressing Jess again.

The children came, eagerly ravenous and bubbling with talk of their secret pool. The four of them sat eating for a time, and meanwhile around them summertime's lingering soft dusk came to gentle the harsh land and lend a roundness to the mountains' sharp curves and angles.

Afterward, they talked for a while, the four of them, then Linda Louise and Billy Ray crawled into quilts upon the earth and instantly fell asleep.

Samuel took the fry pan, the tin plates, and started for the creek. Jess went along with him, explaining how they must travel easterly along the base of the mountains to strike that thoroughfare pass.

"Beyond it lies the village of Hereford and the country of the Absaroka Valley. I'll leave you there, Samuel."

"You aren't able to ride yet," Samuel said, sinking down beside the creek. "If that wound opens again, you may not be so lucky. You could lie out somewhere until you'd bled to death."

"I'll make it all right," Jess said. "What's bothering me is how *you'll* make it."

Samuel scrubbed the dishes and said over his shoulder: "Tell me, what kind of a town is Hereford?"

"It's a town like most other towns. Except that right now it has a problem. Otherwise, it has good stores in it and good people."

"What is its problem?"

"Absaroka Valley is cow country. The cattlemen there have held their ranges against Indians and against outlaws. Now they are trying to hold their land against squatters."

Samuel knew what Jess meant by this. He had encountered the identical condition elsewhere in his endless ramblings.

He said: "The old, old story of the haves standing against the have-nots. Well, we can't stop there either, then."

"Stop there?" asked Jess. "You want to settle?"

"No, not settle. I don't have the time for that. I was thinking of maybe lingering for a few weeks, a couple of months maybe . . . of making friends there . . . getting to know people."

Samuel rose up, brushed sand from his knees, and looked at the scoured plates he held in both hands. He then went on speaking without looking at Jess.

"I must find a place for my children, you see. I've been looking for a long time, but it's always something like this trouble you mentioned. It's always that people are weighted with their own problems, which leaves me still with mine."

Jess leaned there in silver moonlight, his back against a cottonwood tree, his gaze full upon Samuel. After a while he said softly: "Oh, I understand now. I didn't before." He paused briefly before going on in a musing voice. "Try Hereford. Give it a chance. I know the town fairly well. You might find your answer there."

"I think not," replied Samuel, starting back toward the wagon. "Where people are filled with hate, I likely couldn't find the love I'm looking for, Jess."

"Samuel, there is always hate. Maybe that's why you've been on your quest so long. You'll never find a town of people anywhere on earth without hate. What you've got to do is stay in one place long enough to root out the love. It's down there in Hereford. Believe me, I know it is. But you'll have to stay there to find it, not just condemn the place offhand and keep on going."

"No," said Samuel. "I won't leave my children in a place where they'll grow up believing men in wagons and men on horseback are born enemies."

CHAPTER THREE

Jess rode the wagon seat with Samuel guiding him to that forested pass through the mountains. Billy Ray was behind on the black horse, and Linda Louise alternated between poking her head through the canvas behind her father to see what lay ahead, and calling to Billy Ray from the wagon's tailgate, out back.

Behind them, swiftly fading out through trees, lay that long valley they had come down. On both sides stood a blue blur of towering peaks and bristly mountainsides. Directly overhead, but occasionally hidden by giant interlacing stiff-needled tree limbs, was a brassy and faded summertime sky.

Onward lay the wagon trail, mottled and as crooked as some monstrous old snake. The wagon ground along, bouncing, creaking, swaying over stones, and straining up out of chuckholes. Both men upon the high seat sat loosely, riding with each jolt, absorbing the bumps stoically, and keeping their eyes ahead for rocks or deadfall trees which would have to be moved.

Silver-gray clouds of finely rising dust enveloped them when they twice halted to water the stock. Where the pass made its final effort at closing in, the heat was intense. Here too the smell of sweating animals mixed with a stronger smell of alkali earth and baking granite, but only a little distance onward, a reviving freshet of steady breeze came up this soggy canyon to lift their spirits and put spring back into the steps of the mules.

"Not far now," said Jess. "Just around one more bend . . . then you'll see Absaroka Valley."

Samuel made a wan smile. The heat had badly depleted him. He craned for a rearward look at Billy Ray, then settled to his driving again.

They came, as Jess had predicted, around upon the open face of a dark mountain, and below them lay a valley that was nearly heart shaped. Southward, two jutting thrusts of this same mountain chain cut inward upon the valley floor, and northward, the valley gradually closed inward toward the end of that descending road they were upon.

This was a secret place in the dark tangle of a mighty mountain range. The valley was perhaps twenty-five miles in length and not less than five miles wide.

In the heart of it, visible only because sunlight shimmered off tin roofs, was a town. Elsewhere, far out, were the huge old barns— mere specks to Samuel and his children now—of cow ranches. There were two angling watercourses which converged near the town. These glittered with dancing light from amid screenings of great boled cottonwood trees and lacy willow growths.

"It is a fairyland," said Samuel. "It is beautiful."

At his side Jess was gazing from beneath his hat brim out of a sun-darkened, moody face. He said: "The first people to trail cattle in here came over this same trail we're driving over. The Indians brought them here. They were the Bennetts. Abraham and Samantha Bennett. They've been dead thirty years now."

Samuel looked around. "You know the history of the place," he said. "You must know the country quite well."

"I know it," Jess answered. "You see, I was born here. I grew up here."

Samuel kept one foot upon the hand brake to slow his wagon's downward movement, to prevent it from riding up on the mules. He said no more until, much later, they were down from that forested pass and out upon level land where grass grew emerald green and stirrup-high.

Then he said, as they halted to blow the animals: "A man's first love is the land which bore him . . . where he grew up. I was reared in Texas. That was a long time ago, and yet I remember the Pecos and the Staked Plains with a kind of longing." He looped the lines and sat back breathing deeply of cooler, fragrant mountain air.

For a while they sat quietly, with only Linda Louise's piping call to her brother out back intruding upon their private thoughts.

Then Samuel said: "The road beyond . . . out through those yonder mountains . . . must be better than this one we just came over. Is it?"

"It is," replied Jess. "It's wider and much better. That's the road the squatters use to get up in here."

"I see."

"We'd better go along, Samuel. We can make it to Hereford by sundown."

But Samuel was exhausted. "Tomorrow will do as well," he said, and climbed down with some difficulty from the wagon seat, then leaned there, one hand steadying the rest of him upon a wagon wheel, running a practiced eye over this spot where the wagon rested for the means required to make night camp.

Jess also got down. He studied Samuel for a thoughtful time, but this was interrupted when Billy Ray called out to him, saying: "Come on! I'll help you with the mules and the cooking fire."

Linda Louise sprang down and ran up, crying to Jess: "Mr. Black, I'll help in any way I can, too."

Jess laughed as he looked down at her.

It was the first time Samuel had ever seen him smile. And something bitter struck down through Samuel. How could a man whose saddlebags were filled with the sweat-earned money of others find it in his heart and his conscience to laugh?

He watched his son and daughter run on at Jess's side, their voices shrill and pleased. He saw how they strove for the attention of that outlaw, how he looked at them with his quiet smile and his understanding eyes.

Perhaps, thought Samuel, *I should have driven on to this town of Hereford. Perhaps I should wean my Linda Louise and Billy Ray away from this man as quickly as I can.*

And later, while they sat by their little fire, he listened to the legends Jess told his children of the Indians who once had roamed this upland country. Of other stories he told them: stories Samuel had also learned in his own childhood, tales of elves and fairies and angels, of animals that talked and of sly coyotes and wise old owls.

He watched how his little girl's liquid dark eyes, so like her mother's eyes, widened and widened, how they glowed for this man with the tied-down gun. How she hung upon his words, and how Billy Ray sat, elbows upon crossed legs, cupped hands under his jaw, also absorbed and motionless as long as that deep-toned voice ran on.

And Samuel tried seeing past the thin face, the steady gaze, and sun-blackened features of this outlaw, to the heart beyond. He could not, in any conscience at all, condone his suspicions of this man. Still, it puzzled him greatly that Mr. Black could sit as he now sat, hollow cheeks and sunken-set eyes made evil by fire-light, entirely absorbed by the interest of two small children. There could not be all bad in the spirit of such a man.

Then it was over. Jess shooshed the children off to their quilts and turned an easy smile upon Samuel. It was a look both wondering and shadowy with deep understanding.

He said: "Samuel, I want to give Billy Ray the horse."

Samuel sat still.

"Once in every lad's boyhood, he should have an animal he really loves," Jess explained. "It helps him grow up into a better man . . . once the art of loving is learned, Samuel, it never dies."

"No," said Samuel very slowly. "He can't accept your horse. It's impossible."

Jess's smile died slowly. He kept his gray gaze fully upon Samuel. "I had something in mind for Linda Louise too," he said. "I wouldn't have left her out."

"It's not that at all," muttered Samuel, and firmed up under that smoky stare.

"Well, if it's because you think I can't afford . . ."

"Nor that either!" exclaimed Samuel sharply. Then he pushed up off the ground, ran forth a hand to steady himself, and said: "Goodnight."

Jess sat on by the dwindling fire. From time to time, he looked out where shadows were quietly closing down over those two small shapes upon the ground. He heard Samuel pass out away from the wagon westerly, and somewhat later he heard him coughing and gasping and coughing some more.

* * * * *

It was now full night. Jess sat on with the fire's cooling embers for company, turning in his mind grave thoughts. He never afterward recalled falling asleep, how or when he did it. But he never had any difficulty remembering how he came awake—with his heart solidly pounding, with his mind clawing up from stygian blackness to the sound of running animals.

It was something primitive in him which brought him fully upright there by the dead fire, with midnight long past and the cooled out earth sighing around him. Something souring his stomach with fear and anticipation. He blinked away drowsiness and strained to hear again that frightening sound. He placed it before the other noises and the rank scent came along, borne upon a little breeze, and he hurled himself forward with a keening cry. He saw only the ghostly, white bobbing heads, then he was gasping with the pain of his two-handed effort to get the children clear before that stampeding herd of cattle struck.

Something hit his head, turning him over backward, flinging him aside with ease, and he landed close to the wagon, only one leg still protruding out from beneath it. He sank down, down, into a swirling blackness that dripped formlessly until the entire world was buried in it. He lost consciousness.

* * * * *

There was vague dawn light in the purple east when Jess opened his eyes. He felt stickiness along his injured side and put up an exploring hand to see about this. His head hurt with a cadenced pounding, and one leg burned with fire-like intensity. Somewhere close by he heard moaning. He took back a tentative deep breath. There was no wincing pain from his mending ribs. He considered trying to get up but decided for a moment to lie still. The wound along his side had opened somewhat. It was bleeding too, but the entire length of that healing gouge was not opened, and he was thankful for that.

He tried to remember. Something was insistently prodding his thoughts, trying to bring him entirely back to what had happened hours earlier.

He closed his eyes, and water squeezed out under the lids from the headache. There were voices, too. He could hear at least one angry growl rumbling on in a monotonous way. He opened his eyes and moved his head just a little, to get it away from a wagon wheel. In this position he could hear better.

". . . And don't come back," that rumbling voice was telling someone. "If you do you'll never get a second chance. As for your mules . . . we shot 'em. They're dead, granger, so you'll have to leave your wagon. It's worn-out anyway. You aren't losing much. Now get up and put as much of that junk you got as you can carry on your damned back and start walking south. Don't stop. Don't even turn around . . . just keep on walking!"

There came next the sharply striking sound of ridden horses whirling away. That sound gradually fell away, and silence ensued. But only for a second. Jess heard that same pitiful moaning again. He got both elbows back and pushed, heaved himself half-up off the ground beneath the wagon.

It all came back then—the instinctive warning that had awakened him, his lunge to save the children, the blackness afterward.

Out a short distance, Samuel was down on both knees. His back was bowed, and he weaved gently back and forth. In front of him, scarcely visible to Jess, was the very still form of Linda Louise. Even as Jess's vision cleared, in the new day's sparkling brightness, he saw that bloody mat of taffy hair, the churned earth, and the shredded quilts that had been Linda Louise's bed. He also saw where one foot lay, unnaturally twisted, and onward another ten feet what remained of the shoe off that foot.

Jess took a long breath and began working his slow way from beneath the wagon. He touched something that gave at his contact and looked over. Billy Ray was there, dry-eyed, white from throat to eyes, staring out at his father and sister in a stupor.

Jess got clear. He swayed up to his feet in the curdling quietude. This effort was too much. His head swam, and his vision blurred out. He flung forth a seeking hand, found a wheel, and bent upon it, hanging there with air passing in, passing out, until steadiness returned. Then he swung his head upward, saw the mules lying dead, side by side. He saw the utter devastation that stampeding herd of cattle had made of their camp and took a step forward.

It must have been this sudden movement that broke Billy Ray out of his trance, for when Jess's leg moved, the lad gave a scream and flung himself onward where his father knelt. He pounded the ground raising a dust. He flung his body about, and he kept at his screaming.

Samuel heeded none of this. He continued to kneel there, weaving back and forth and softly moaning. It was, in Jess's ears, a terrible sound, because it came from deep in the throat of a grown man.

Jess looked for his black horse and did not see him. He returned his attention to those other forms down in the torn earth. He went forward, caught Billy Ray, and pulled him bodily upright. He turned the boy, shook him with one hand until Billy Ray's noise ceased and a tremor passed over him from head to toes, leaving him afterward hanging in Jess's hands.

"Listen to me," the man said. "Billy Ray, listen to me. You'll have to do this on foot. The mules are dead, and my horse is gone." He gave another sharp shake. "You run south from here, and keep going until you come to the first ranch. Do you hear me, boy?"

"Y-es. Yes, I hear you."

"Bring back help. Bring back a wagon and some men."

Jess spun the lad, gave him a forward, rough push. "Go now, and send someone for the doctor at Hereford."

"I'll . . . I'll get lost."

"No," said Jess. "Keep going due south. There is a big ranch no more than two miles from this camp."

"But they might shoot me. They might . . ."

"They won't do any such thing, Billy Ray. Listen, boy, we need help badly. We need that doctor from Hereford." Jess took two steps toward the lad. "You hurry now, and when you get to that place, you tell the folks there Jess sent you. Tell them to hurry up here."

Billy Ray gulped and sniffled, put a lingering look upon his father's moving back, and then he started to run, swiftly and more swiftly, heading south through the tall grass shining with dew.

Jess watched him until he was beyond sight, then went outward where Samuel was down on his knees. He moved out around so that he could see Linda Louise better, and he knelt beside her, reaching forward to arrange her arms and legs naturally, to turn her up on her back and smooth away her blood-matted hair. He shifted a little, when the sun came rushing over the land, to shield her face from those lemony yellow rays, and that was when he saw her lips quiver and her eyelids flicker.

He held his breath, staring, then went swiftly down to put his ear upon her chest. "She's alive," he croaked to Samuel. "She's alive, man. Get some blankets and some water!"

CHAPTER FOUR

It was three hours past sunup when the riders came whirling up, bearing with them Billy Ray. Jess had made a soft pallet under the wagon away from the sun for Linda Louise. He and Samuel had cleansed her wounds and bathed her face. Beyond that there was nothing they could do for her. Samuel stayed with her, his big, bony frame telescoped into awkward smallness beneath the wagon.

Jess, much revived, walked with short steps back and forth, pausing now and then to look southward, to listen. Impatience and a sense of personal futility rode his spirit hard, until those horsemen came racing up, seven of them, all armed and capable-looking men, with one of them carrying Billy Ray behind his saddle.

The foremost of these men was grizzled and gray. He left his horse as it slid to a halt and, racing toward Jess, thrust a gloved hand out, crying loudly: "By God, we thought you were dead.

Pete and Jonas were killed, and those folks up north said you probably were dead, too, although they never found your body in the mountains."

Jess made no reply to all this. He shook the grizzled man's fist then dropped it. "Did you send someone to town for the doctor, John?"

"Yes. We weren't sure what was wrong. That kid was pretty bad off when he got to the ranch. But we sent for him anyway."

"Where's the wagon I told the lad to have you fetch back with you?"

"It's coming, Jess. We came on ahead. What's the matter, exactly?" The weathered-looking older man turned his head left to right. "Who killed those mules? Who's that under the old wagon yonder?"

"These folks found me, John. They patched me up and brought me with them southward. Last night we were hit by driven cattle. The little girl was run over. She's bad off. Dying, I think."

"A little kid?" said the grizzled man.

"Eight years old."

"Who done it, Jess?"

"I'm not sure. I got knocked out. But I heard a voice this morning when I came around."

"Whose voice?"

"Never mind that for now. Send someone back to bring on that damned wagon. Send another man to catch the doctor and detour him to the Big B."

The older man turned, bawled out some names, and sent a brace of horsemen running south. He then crossed to where Jess stood with one hand upon Billy Ray's shoulders, got down upon one knee, and craned for a long look under the wagon. He withdrew slowly, pale in the face, and regained his feet. When he put his gaze upon Jess, it was ironlike.

"One thing to run 'em off," he growled. "Another thing to do . . . this."

Jess said nothing.

After a while the grizzled man, looking Jess up and down, said in a quieter way: "You look like hell, boy. You need a shave, and you've lost twenty pounds." He pulled at his rider's doeskin gloves after saying this. There was very clearly something else on his mind. He said haltingly and softly: "Did you save any of it, Jess?"

"I saved all of it, John. It's in my saddlebags."

John relaxed his full length. He turned, as did the others standing there, at the onward sound of a wagon's approach.

When this vehicle came up, Jess said loudly to the remaining riders: "You boys stay here. See that no one bothers these folks' belongings. I'll send back another team from the ranch. Then you fetch along their stuff."

The cowboys began to drift away. Some stood silently considering the dead mules. Others backtracked that torn earth to the place where those stampeding cattle had been bunched for the charge over Samuel's camp.

John Burr, foreman of the Big B cattle outfit, beckoned the driven wagon up close, then said to its driver: "Give us a hand, Mike. There's a hurt little girl here. We got to get her back to the ranch."

They made a thick pallet and with great gentleness lifted her, put her into the ranch wagon, erected a shade to keep out the sun, and looked at one another. These were hard men. Not a one of them standing there at this time had not fought his share of battles. But this was something else. This standing helplessly gazing upon a whimpering child with a broken body and the slowly spreading paleness of death in her cheeks.

Jess went up beside Samuel. He put out a hand to mildly shake the ill man, to bring his attention around.

"You ride with her," he said. "They've been instructed to go slow and be easy. Get up in the wagon with her, Samuel."

Billy Ray sidled up and put a hand into Jess's hand. He stood like that, looking dry-eyed where his sister lay. Samuel moved; he went unsteadily forward. John Burr and another cowman assisted him into the wagon. Someone placed a folded blanket for Samuel to sit upon.

"Jess . . .?"

Those holding, sweaty fingers drew Jess's attention downward. "Yes, son?"

"Me, too? Can I ride with them, too?"

Instead of answering, Jess led Billy Ray to the tailgate. "Give Billy Ray a hand up," he said.

John Burr's big arms went out, downward, then upward in one powerful swing, depositing Billy Ray at his sister's side. Burr nodded, and the wagon began a big arcing turnaround.

Jess and John Burr stood together, watching as the wagon slowly headed out. Around them were five silent range men. Every eye followed the slow and careful progress of that wagon until it was well down the land, then Burr said: "Jessie boy, it's been a month. Things been gettin' worse in the valley. I guess we both know who did this thing. At least we know who runs this upper end of the valley. But like I said . . . things been gettin' worse."

Jess turned his sober gaze upon the older man. His tone was bitter when he said: "They must be worse, John, because I never heard of the cattlemen taking the war to eight-year-old girls before."

"They probably didn't know," said Burr. "You say they hit you after midnight?"

"John, you know how that's done. First, they scout up the settler camp, count the guns in it and the people. Then they give one strong warning. Then, if the warning doesn't work, they drive 'em out."

Burr said, a little lamely: "Tempers are gettin' pretty short, Jessie. Dozens more of these wagoners have come into the valley this past month, since you been away."

"That's no excuse, John. She is just a little girl."

Burr nodded at this, lowered his eyes, and tugged absently at his gloves. Then he looked up again and changed the subject. "Your ma will surely be glad to see you. She believed like the rest of us . . . that you were dead. You want to head back now? We got an extra saddle horse."

Jess turned slowly to survey the wreckage around them. His gaze lingered longest where those wise old mules lay swelling in the sunlight. "Yeah," he said in hard-toned bitterness. "Let's go home, John."

* * * * *

They rode along, the two of them, following in the wake of that ranch wagon. Behind them remained three Big B cowboys to guard Samuel's pitiful possessions.

They came down behind the wagon where it was making its slow but steady progress and rode back a hundred yards seeing the tousle-headed boy and the bowed man.

John Burr said: "Who are they, Jess?"

"It's too long a story for now," came back the reply to this. "But they aren't squatters. They were just passing through."

"They picked a bad time for that," mused Burr, "and they picked a bad way to do it . . . comin' on in that old wagon for all the world lookin' like squatters."

Jess said quickly, on a flare of hot temper: "How else could they have come on, John? All they had was those two old mules . . . that worn-out old wagon."

Burr went silent.

They passed onto a sanded wide roadway and turned westward to go along following this as far as the mighty log gateway into a ranch. Burned deeply into an overhead crossbar at this gate was a cattle brand: one big letter B.

John Burr put a sidling glance from beneath his hat brim at Jess when they entered here. He seemed on the verge of saying something, but the younger man's stone-set expression deterred him.

Onward a quarter mile was a prosperous set of ranch buildings in a setting of huge cottonwoods. The central residence here was long and low, with a covered porch that ran along the entire north-facing front of the house. Some distance from this house were two huge log barns. Closer to the house was a log bunkhouse, also with a covered porch. Between those big barns was a network of pole corrals large enough to hold a thousand cattle at a time.

A man and woman were moving from the central house out into the yard as Jess, John Burr, and that swaying wagon approached.

Jess threw them a long look, then wheeled out around the wagon and loped ahead. John saw him alight, saw Jess and the woman come swiftly together in hot sunlight, and also watched as the other man hobbled up with a stiffly extended arm and a wide, wide grin.

Burr smiled softly.

When the wagon halted and the driver got down to go along the side, those other three people moved forward also. Jess was speaking swiftly as the three of them came up. He stopped when Burr came around to take his saddle horse. The woman, as gray as Burr himself was, stood stock-still staring down into the wagon. Burr heard her breath catch up, heard her deep sigh follow that. Then she was herself again.

Turning upon Jess and the other men, she said swiftly: "Bring her into the house." When the cowboy who had tooled the wagon bent to reach for Linda Louise, the older woman's tongue lashed him.

"Not like that, Slim. All of you . . . John, come here. Now then, all of you take hold of that pallet like it was a stretcher. Jessie, not with one hand."

"He's hurt," explained Burr. "He's been shot. He can't use both hands, ma'am."

"Then let the others do it, Jessie." She directed the men, indicating with a pointed finger where each should stand. "All right, gently now. John, be careful. Don't bump the tailgate with her. Fine. Now come along with me."

They moved through fierce sunlight with their small burden, taking short steps and trailing the woman. Jess remained by the wagon. He felt weak, suddenly, drained-dry and weak. The yard around was utterly silent. The same damp hand crept into his again that had sought him out once before back at the camp. He squeezed those thin fingers before looking down.

"Will she be all right?" Billy Ray asked, pale eyes full of trouble, full of bewilderment. "Jess, why did those men run their cattle over us?"

Jess said nothing.

Behind him, from within the wagon, came the thick, dull tone of Samuel. "Yes, why did they, Jess? Because they thought we were more squatters? But why didn't they ask who we were first?" Samuel eased himself down carefully over the tailgate. He put out a hand to steady himself and stared hot-eyed toward that big, rambling house into which his daughter had been carried. "Are these the people you told me of . . . the people with love in their hearts?"

Samuel's voice dropped away, and the silence ran on for a while.

John Burr reappeared upon that yonder porch. He was donning his hat and standing over there gazing outward at Jess, at Samuel, at young Billy Ray. He stepped down into the yard and slow-paced his way forward. He did not speak when he was close. Instead, he put a pained gaze upon Billy Ray, then upon Samuel. Lastly, he looked at Jess.

"You better go get cleaned up," he murmured. "Your ma'll want to talk to you, Jess. By the way, where's your saddle?"

"Back at the camp."

"We forgot it," said John, his attention closing down upon this.

"It's not important, John," Jess told him.

"No, I reckon not. Anyway, the men'll be guardin' it up there." Burr turned this over in his mind a moment, then blew out a big sigh, saying: "All the same I think I'd better go fetch those saddle-bags home."

"First, fix Samuel and Billy Ray with bunks," ordered Jess. "They'll want to clean up, too. Afterward, show them where Linda Louise is. They'll want to know that for certain."

John nodded.

CHAPTER FIVE

Jess was in the main house a long time, and when he finally emerged, he came upon Samuel and Billy Ray standing silently upon the porch.

Samuel did not look up as Jess came forward, but Billy Ray did. His pale eyes, still with their bewilderment, lingered upon Jess, seeing that he had shaved and that his clothing was fresh and clean.

"That woman won't let us see Linda Louise," the boy said to Jess.

For a long time, Jess simply looked far out without speaking. There was impatience in his face. Then he said to Billy Ray: "She's resting now. She needs all the rest she can get right now, son. It's the most important thing at a time like this. You understand?"

Billy Ray understood. He looked around at his father.

Samuel let himself down into a chair. He still did not look at Jess.

From down the yard, a man's bull-bass voice fluted outward in a loud call. Jess swiftly turned, saw an oncoming rig, and went quickly down toward where it would wheel across the yard. John Burr too came trotting.

The rig halted, gentle dust rose around it. Immediately, Jess began pulling insistently at the sleeve of the man who remained in this buggy.

"Hurry up, Doc. It's a little girl. She's inside with my mother."

The older man, lean and spare and wearing an acid expression, got down from his buggy.

"Let go my arm," he snapped at Jess. "I'm moving as fast as I can." He reached into the buggy and lifted a black satchel from the floorboards, then squinted upward. "What happened to her? Who is she, anyway?"

"A stampede went over her," said Jess. "What difference does it make who she is, she needs you."

John Burr put his unwavering stare upon the doctor. "Talk later," he said shortly, and bobbed his head toward the house.

Under this strong inducement, the medical man went forward annoyedly. He shot Samuel and Billy Ray a look when he reached the porch, then pushed on into the house.

John Burr called toward the barn. When a cowboy appeared, he said: "Take care of Doc's rig."

Jess stood a moment longer in the hot sunlight. Then he said: "I thought you were going after the saddlebags."

"I was. I was saddlin' up when Doc came along."

"Take someone with you. And have them lead a team to bring back the old wagon."

"Yes," said Burr, sounding as though he had planned doing this anyway. "Jess, you better have Doc take a look at you, too."

They were parting from one another, each heading across the yard in different directions, when a body of horsemen swept into sight passing along the ranch road.

John Burr halted the second he glimpsed these newcomers.

As recognition came, he twisted to call to Jess: "Mike Slattery and his crew!"

Jess watched those horsemen, then went back down where Burr stood. "They've got my black horse," he said.

Burr nodded. His next words were dryly said: "I reckon we know where they got him, too."

The riders slowed where they wheeled across toward Jess and John Burr. Their leader was a red-faced, redheaded, large man with flashing dark eyes and a look of violence to him. He hailed Jess with something like surprise in his tone, then, half twisting in his saddle, he said: "Give him his black horse."

John Burr moved up to take the lead rope. He looked from the horse to Mike Slattery, then drifted his careful look on to where Jess stood.

"Where did you find him?" Jess asked the red-faced mounted man. "At that camp you drove your cattle over last night, Mike?"

Slattery put both hands upon his saddle horn. He regarded Jess for a moment of thoughtful silence before speaking. Then he said: "It was dark, Jess. Were you at that camp too?"

"I was."

"Well, hell . . . we didn't know. We'd heard you got killed along with two of your Big B riders up north. In fact, your horse trailed us after we left. Not until this mornin', when some o' my boys saw the brand on that horse, did we know it belonged to you. Then we come right over here to tell your ma a bunch of murderin' squatters had him." Slattery made a hard little smile. "And here you are, big as life and plumb alive."

"I thought that was you last night, Mike."

Slattery sat on, putting his careful, his wary and truculent stare upon Jess, saying nothing.

"Anyone else would've warned them first. Not you, you've got that kind of a reputation in the valley."

"Hold on a minute!" exclaimed the red-faced man, his tone changing, becoming rough. "I might ask what the hell you were doin' ridin' with squatters. You're the biggest cowman in these parts, Jess. You got no business with those people."

"They kept me alive after I was shot, Mike. You could've found that out if you'd ridden in first, instead of acting like a savage."

Slattery's face hardened against Jess. "You ought to mind your tongue a little," he said. "To me a squatter is a squatter, and I don't give a damn who's ridin' with him."

"Those people weren't squatters. They were just passing through."

"With a wagon and a team?"

"Squatters aren't the only folks who travel that way, Mike. I want to tell you something else. If that little girl dies, I'm going to personally see to it that you pay damned dear for what you did."

Slattery's brows drew inward and downward. The riders bunched up around him also looked puzzled.

"What little girl?" Slattery demanded.

"Her name is Linda Louise Patton. She is eight years old. I tried to pull her clear when you drove your cattle over the camp, but I couldn't. Then I got knocked out by a critter. She's in the house now, Mike, and Doc is with her. Your stampede went over her."

Slattery sat up there, wearing his frown and saying nothing until he'd digested this. "I didn't see any little girl. Anyway, those damned people got to be taught Absaroka Valley's for cow outfits only."

John Burr now spoke forth from where he stood, still holding the lead rope to Jess's black horse. "That doesn't sound much like you're sorry," he said to Slattery, his gaze fixed upward. "She was just a little kid."

"Mind your own business," snapped Slattery. "You're only Big B's foreman, so keep in your place."

Burr's grizzled, sunblasted countenance gradually darkened with hot blood. He said: "Mike, you get down . . ."

But Slattery was speaking again, addressing himself once more to Jess. "I didn't know about the kid. I told you that. It was an accident. You can't hold me responsible if she dies anyway. It was dark last night, Jess."

"I'll hold you responsible, Mike, whether she dies or not. Why did you shoot their mules?"

"Jess, this is war with these people. Us cowmen got to bury the sword in 'em to the hilt. Otherwise, they'll keep comin', keep squattin' on our land. We got to make it so harsh for 'em, they'll be glad to get out . . . and they'll tell others to steer wide around Absaroka Valley."

Jess was mutely staring at big Mike Slattery. The flash of those dark eyes, the bear-trap set to Slattery's mouth, his unrelenting toughness, kept Jess from saying anything more for a long time.

Slattery glared downward, giving look for look. Then he loosened in his saddle, his expression altered to a look of irony. He said, more quietly but with unmistakable bitterness: "The innocent sometimes get hurt in wars. But that's not important. What I'm beginnin' to wonder about, Jess, is just where you stand in all this? Maybe those people saved your life . . . maybe they nursed you along, like you say. But they got no business in here, squatters or no. But here you are, standin' up for them. Makes me wonder which side you're actually on, Jess. There'll be other cowmen in the valley who'll also want to know."

"You know where I stand," replied Jess tartly. "Right where Big B has always stood. I'm against anyone who comes in here and tries to preempt Big B's deeded land. But I never tried to kill those squatters. Least of all I never made war against little eight-year-old girls."

"I told you, dammit, I didn't know anything about a little kid!"

"Then why didn't you ride up and talk to 'em first? That's always been the way, Mike."

"To hell with 'em," snarled Slattery. "They're scum. I don't have to talk to 'em."

"This time you should have. They weren't squatters."

"That don't mean a damned thing, Jess."

John Burr made a hopeless gesture with his free hand. Jess saw this; he felt the same way. There was no point in trying to reason with Slattery. He turned upon his heel and started away.

For a moment Slattery watched Jess's moving shoulders, then he said curtly: "All right, Jess. I flipped the coin, and you called it. You're on the side of the squatters. Now we'll see how that boot fits with the other ranchers in the valley."

Jess halted and turned.

Slattery hauled his mount around, barked at the cowboys with him, and the lot of them went thundering back out of Big B's yard the same way they had come in.

Jess went slowly back to the verandah. There he found Samuel's wondering gaze upon him. He leaned upon an upright log staring out where the diminishing dust cloud was thinning.

Samuel said: "I heard most of it. I thought you were an outlaw."

Jess swung his head. "An outlaw?"

Samuel looked away. "I went through your saddlebags, trying to find out anything about you. They were full of money. I thought you had robbed a stage or a bank."

Jess continued to stare at Samuel. Then he said quietly: "I didn't explain because of that money. I was helpless in your hands, Samuel. I didn't know what might happen if you knew about the money." He took a big breath. "I'm Jess Bennett of the Big B. My grandfather was that same Bennett I told you about who first brought cattle into Absaroka Valley. That woman who is caring for Linda

Louise is my mother. My pa is dead . . . he died six years back. This is my ranch." Jess looked at Billy Ray, then back to Samuel. "An outlaw . . ." he murmured to himself, shaking his head.

"I'm sorry," muttered Samuel. "It was the way you wore your gun, the quality of the horse you rode."

"Samuel, I went up the trail with seven hundred prime steers with two Big B riders. I sold the critters, collected my money, and started for home. I was attacked by men who somehow knew I had all that money. My two men were killed, and I was shot. You know the rest. I kept going as long as I could. Then you found me."

Billy Ray sniffled. This noise brought his father's anguished eyes around. Beyond Billy Ray stood Jess, looking downward where Samuel sat.

"A man makes mistakes," said Samuel slowly. "He spends his life balancing between what he thinks is right and what he imagines might be wrong. I didn't know what to do about you. I thought we might eventually come to a town, and I'd turn you over to some sheriff."

"Then why did you hide the wagon every time we made camp?" asked Jess. "I thought you did that because you were planning something . . . because you didn't want interference in case you made up your mind to kill me."

"No," stated Samuel, looking rueful now. "I did that because I thought a posse was after you. I figured even an outlaw deserved a chance for his life, Jess."

They stared at one another.

Jess said finally, softly: "I'll be damned."

"Caution can be worse than frankness, can't it?" asked Samuel, his gaze seeking forgiveness for his erroneous thoughts.

Jess smiled. "An honest heart is better than both," he said. "You're a good man, Samuel. I don't forget a debt."

At this juncture the door opened, the doctor emerged, and looked at Jess with a grave expression.

"Is this the girl's father?" he asked of Jess, speaking of Linda Louise, and when Jess nodded, his face tightening, the doctor turned a little so that he was facing Samuel. "Your little girl has a broken ankle, a crushed chest, and a fractured skull."

He paused to shift his attention back to Jess. "Is this man a person I can talk to?" he asked.

Jess said: "Tell him the whole truth, Doc."

The medical man turned, closed the door behind him, and spoke once more to Samuel, his tone quiet and his expression grave.

"It is very unlikely that she will survive her injuries. God knows, I don't think she will. She is young and strong, yes, but she is badly hurt. I'll do all in my power for her. She cannot be moved for at least a month . . . if ever. But don't fret over that, sir. She couldn't be in better hands."

The doctor went along to the very edge of the porch. He teetered there, holding his black satchel heavily, and from the corner of his bitter lips, he said to Jess: "I'm going to send Sheriff Richards out here, Jess. The man responsible for this ought to be drawn and quartered." He stepped down into the hot sunlight and slowly passed onward toward the barn where his buggy had been parked.

Upon the porch there was not a sound until Samuel began rocking back and forth in his chair. This steady squeak touched down into Jess like scraping steel fingernails. He turned to enter the house, saw Billy Ray's swimming eyes upon him, and took the little boy's hand, drawing him along, taking him away from that rocking, unseeing man who sat on, entirely unconscious of their presence.

CHAPTER SIX

Jess and Billy Ray tiptoed into the room where Linda Louise lay. Mary Bennett, Jess's mother, sat by the bed, gazing downward. She raised her eyes when Jess and Linda Louise's brother came up.

"She's resting. Doctor Hartman gave her something." Mary looked at Billy Ray for a moment, then put out a cool hand and drew the boy to her. She held him close to her and stroked his hair, saying gently: "You can help your sister, son. Pray for her." Then she looked upward speaking in a different tone. "Did Mike Slattery do this, son?"

Jess nodded. He was gazing upon the small outline in that big bed. "He was just here . . . brought back my horse." Jess looked at his mother. "He said he didn't know there was a little girl at the wagon."

Mary Bennett sat on, stroking Billy Ray's head saying nothing, her face sad and her gray eyes, like her son's eyes, turning bleak under the motivation of her thoughts. Then she got up and took

Billy Ray's hand. "You'll be hungry," she said to the boy. "Come along, I know what little boys like to eat." She swung her glance to Jess, considered his wasted look, and said: "You could stand some fattening up, too."

"How about Linda Louise?" asked Jess, hovering at the bedside.

"She'll sleep for a long time. Come along you two. We'll leave her alone."

They passed through several large, silent rooms to emerge into a spacious kitchen. Here, the crippled older man, the one who had greeted Jess upon his return to Big B at his mother's side, was busy over a large wood range. He looked around, then made a slow smile, saying: "Sit down, Jess. Danged if you don't look like a gutted snowbird. Must've lost twenty, thirty pounds." The cook's wise old eyes fell upon Billy Ray. His smile widened. "I got just the stuff for growin' cowboys, too . . . chocolate cookies fresh baked."

Jess pulled Billy Ray down beside him. They began eating.

Mary Bennett said to her son: "How about the father? Will he want to eat something?"

"I think the best thing to do right now is leave him alone," replied Jess. "He's on the porch."

The cook turned this over in his mind, then he said: "Never was a time o' trouble when a man couldn't do with a cup of fresh coffee. I'll take some out to him."

Mary Bennett also sat, but she did not eat. She said: "Jess, where is the money from the cattle?"

"John went after it. It's in my saddlebags."

"What happened, son?"

"Slattery drove a herd over . . ."

"No, I meant to you and Jonas and Pete."

"Oh. We delivered the cattle without any trouble. I got the money, and we started back. About ten miles south of Cedarville, we were ambushed by four men. They got Pete the first volley. Jonas and I tried to make a fight of it. They got Jonas. Then I tried to make a running fight of it. I shot one of them, but when he hit the ground, he shot upward and got me along the side. After that, I don't remember very much. I recollect getting into a forest and my horse running until he was run out. There was a creek . . . I remember hearing water. The next thing I knew, this boy's father here . . . Samuel Patton . . . had me in his wagon all bandaged up, and we were coming south. That's all, Ma."

"How badly were you hurt?"

"Couple busted ribs and a pretty long gash where the slug angled upward from my waist damned near to my shoulder. It's healing well though, and the ribs are just about mended."

"This Samuel Patton saved your life?"

Jess nodded and arose. He had caught the sound of horsemen passing over the yard. His mother saw how Billy Ray looked around as Jess arose. Smiling, she said to Billy Ray: "You just sit there and eat. Jess will be around when you're finished."

The sound of the riders beyond drew Jess out into the yard. John Burr was dismounting before the house. He tossed Jess the scuffed and bulging saddlebags.

"All there," he said, then jerked his head at the second man, who was also dismounting. "Met the sheriff at the gate. Brought him on in with me."

Jess nodded, waited for the lanky, quiet man at Burr's side to finish with his animal, then he said: "Doc didn't waste any time, Sheriff. He said he was going to send you out here."

"I was comin' anyway," responded the man, placing his back to his horse and drifting his gaze onward past Jess to where Samuel sat, still rocking. "Met Doc a couple miles from here, and he told me about the little girl." Now, Sheriff Blaine Richards brought his grave glance back to Jess. "Doc was pretty worked up. It seems he's for tarring and feathering someone. Jess, do you know who that someone was?"

Jess hefted the saddlebags. He was conscious of Samuel nearby. He said: "Come on, Sheriff. Let's walk down to the barn."

They went away from the house. As they paced along, Jess told of Mike Slattery's visit to Big B. Of Slattery's unrelenting attitude.

Blaine Richards listened, saying nothing. He was a spare man with words, but when he had something to say, he said it. At the barn he halted to cool his face with water scooped from a trough. Then he perched upon the edge of that trough and very carefully twisted up a smoke. When he had this lighted, he said: "Mike's got the others pretty fired up, Jess. There's been some real trouble since you went north."

"What kind of trouble, Blaine?"

"Night riding. Masked horsemen running cattle over squatter's camp, puttin' the torch to their tents and wagons. Shootin' their teams."

"Slattery . . .?"

Blaine Richards shrugged. "No identification. They come in fast, raise hell, and race away. So far no one's got a good look at 'em." The sheriff raised his calm eyes. "Sure it's Slattery . . . but I can't prove it. Besides, those people are squatters. They move onto a cowman's range and set up their camps. You know that land's all deeded, Jess. They got no right to do that on deeded land. It's not like they were homesteaders. These people are just plain preemptors. They're tryin' to steal patented land, which is absolutely illegal."

"But that doesn't give Mike the right to try and kill them."

"No," drawled Blaine Richards, "it doesn't. Only, Mike and most of the other cowmen think it does." Richards tossed down his smoke. He ground it out under a booted foot. "It's a damned mess any way you look at it, Jess. One of these days, this thing that

happened to that little girl was bound to happen. I been expectin'
it for a long time." Richards got up off the water trough. "Maybe
you can reason with the cowmen. I've tried, and I got nowhere. I
think, though, that they might listen to you."

"I'll make the rounds," said Jess.

Blaine Richards gazed over towards the verandah. "Who is
that?" he asked, indicating Samuel Patton with a thrust of his chin.
"The little girl's pa?"

"Yes. Their name is Patton. They weren't squatting, Blaine.
They were passing through on their way south."

Sheriff Richards shook his head. "Sometimes that's the way it
goes," he mused. "The innocent get caught in the middle. Damn
Slattery anyway. Doc told me how bad off the little girl is."

"If she dies, I'm going after him, Blaine."

Richards swung his head and studied Jess's expression, then
he sighed. "More trouble. Listen, let me handle it this time. I'll
get up a warrant against Mike and bring him to trial. The circuit
judge'll be through here next month. Maybe a stiff fine'll calm
him down a little."

Jess stood in the shade of the barn, turning this over in his
mind. If he intended to speak, he did not get the opportunity,
for at this juncture John Burr emerged from the bunkhouse calling over to Jess: "Riders coming! Looks like some of the ranchers
from south o' here."

It was. Four men came riding stiffly into the glittering yard,
their shaded faces glum-looking, their moving eyes taking in Sheriff Blaine Richards standing there with Jess. As they reined down,
John Burr drifted closer, becoming busy where a corral stringer was
broken, his head cocked to hear.

The speaker for these four men was a young man about Jess's
own age. He was very dark, possibly with a taint of Indian blood,
and he had a tough face. His name was Hugh Shannon, owner of

the Rafter S outfit. His squinted black eyes were grave, and the tilt of a high-bridged nose gave him the look of a man rock-like in his convictions.

He nodded at Blaine Richards and Jess, then he said: "Glad to see you're all right, Jess."

"Thanks," answered Jess, and waited.

The three other mounted men were older, but in each of their faces was the same resolute, tough expression. They also nodded, murmuring greetings. Then they became silent, and Jess got the feeling that this was all prearranged; that the others had elected Hugh Shannon their spokesman.

Shannon said: "We just had a talk with Mike, Jess." He let that lie there between them for a moment, his voice short, holding many things back.

Jess was conscious of the strain there in the yard with them. He had known Hugh Shannon since boyhood. Shannon was a man who held himself severely in check. He never bluffed and he was absolutely trustworthy.

"He told us you came back with a family of squatters."

"They aren't squatters, Hugh. They are folks passing through on their way south."

The four tough faces did not alter. Jess knew then that Mike had also said this to them. He could imagine how Slattery had slyly made something else out of it. Resentment against Slattery began to firm up in him all over again.

"Did he tell you fellows about driving a herd over their camp and nearly killing a little girl?"

Shannon looked past at the sheriff. He seemed wary now and unwilling to open up in Richards's presence. He said: "He didn't admit doin' anything, Jess. He only said you were takin' the side of the squatters now."

"He's a damned liar, and he knows it."

Shannon shifted on leather. He looked around at his companions. They were watching Jess and Blaine Richards.

One of them, old Clem Brite of the Ox-Yoke outfit, said: "Jess, all you got to do is tell us pointblank you ain't for the squatters, and we'll accept that."

"I'll tell you that," answered Jess. "But I'm surprised that you'd ask it, Clem. I'm not for the squatters. I never have been. What possible reason would I have to help people who come here to steal our land? Hell, Big B's got more deeded range than any of you. What you're suspecting me of doesn't make sense, and you know it."

Hugh Shannon murmured: "I didn't think it made sense, Jess. But a feller can't always figure how another man's mind works."

"I'll tell you how Slattery's mind works!" exclaimed Jess tartly. "I told him that if that little girl dies, I'm holding him personally responsible. I meant that, and he knows I meant it. So, he's starting this talk of me siding with the squatters for just one reason. He wants to make you cowmen suspicious of me. He wants you on his side if the little girl dies and I go after him."

Shannon sat still, gazing downward at Jess in a solemnly thoughtful way. Finally, shifting his attention, he said to Sheriff Richards: "What's your position in this, Blaine?"

Richards gazed unwaveringly upon the four mounted men when he gave his answer. "I've about got the last of those preemptors cleaned out of the valley. You don't have any left on your land, have you, Clem?"

Brite shook his head.

"You, Hugh?"

"No."

"You other fellows?"

The remaining ranchers also shook their heads without speaking.

"Then you know where I stand. I'm against illegality whether squatters are guilty . . . or you men are guilty. I understand how you feel, and I can't say as I blame you a lot. But stampedin' cattle over folks and maybe killin' them in the process puts you down to the level of land stealers. When you do that, then I'm plumb against you." Richards ran his calm blue gaze back over those four faces again, and added: "You boys wouldn't want partial law. I know every blessed one of you. You're fair and honest and decent men. You want protection under the law, not persecution or murder. That's what I'm workin' day an' night to give you. All right?"

Hugh Shannon took up his reins. "All right," he said, and started to wheel his horse.

Jess halted him with words. "Hugh, don't let Slattery edge you into anything. He's making a crusade out of his hatred for squatters. Don't let him carry you along with him."

Shannon did not reply to this, but he nodded his head. Then he led his companions out of Big B's yard in an easy lope.

Blaine Richards watched those four riders fade out through the shimmering heat. He spoke a mild curse and eased back down upon the water trough, putting a wry look over where John Burr was still fiddling with the broken corral stringer.

"John, you fixed an' unfixed that cussed pole so many times, it's about worn smooth from handling."

Big B's foreman straightened up, grinning. He strolled forward to stop beside Jess. "Why," he said to them both, "doesn't Mike just ride in here, say he's sorry for what he did, and act like a man should act?"

"Because he's big Mike Slattery," grunted Jess, "and big Mike Slattery fancies himself king of Absaroka Valley."

"Funny thing about kings," drawled Sheriff Richards. "They keep gettin' tumbled off their thrones. It happens right along."

He straightened up off the trough again. "Well, I got to get back to town."

"You goin' to swear out that warrant for Slattery?"

"Yep. Goin' to serve it on him this afternoon. See you boys later."

CHAPTER SEVEN

All the stars were brilliant in the sky that night. Daytime heat was past, and a sickle-moon rode serenely overhead. From down by the bunkhouse, there came the soft sound of someone playing a guitar. Billy Ray and Jess sat upon the verandah up at the main house. Samuel was abed, and Jess's mother was maintaining her vigil with Linda Louise.

"A lot can happen in a couple of days," said Jess to the boy. "Can't it?"

Billy Ray bobbed his unruly haired head up and down. He said: "Pa acts strange, Jess. He just sets there looking off into space."

Jess cocked an eye at that pewter moon. He said: "Want to take a ride, Billy Ray?"

"On horseback?" came the piping, quick, and interested reply. "Sure. Where to, Jess?"

They rose up simultaneously. Jess grinned downward. "Just around," he said. "It's a wonderful night. Come on."

They went along to the barn, and Jess gravely brought forth his black horse, rigged it out, and tossed the split reins to Billy Ray. He afterward brought out a solid short-backed Appaloosa horse, put his own outfit on this animal, and led it out into the softly lighted yard.

"Mount up," he said, swinging over leather, and afterward, as they were riding northwest beyond the home place, he said: "That's a good name you gave the horse you're riding, Billy Ray."

"Big Black?"

"Yeah. He's big, and he's sure enough black. Tell you what. You keep him."

Billy Ray stopped in his tracks. He put a wondering wide gaze over at Jess. "You mean . . . Big Black?"

"Yes. He's yours from now on."

". . . Jess?"

Hearing the quick, sucked-back breath, the shakiness of Billy Ray's voice, Jess rode on saying: "There are times in a fellow's life when human friends just aren't enough. He needs an animal to talk to. Come on, let's lope a little."

They ran on for a mile, then Jess slowed to throw a careful look around. Billy Ray was all right now. The sniffles were gone, and his eyes were bright and shiny, no longer misty or wet.

He caught Jess watching him and said: "I thank you. I don't know what else to say."

Jess smiled. His teeth whitely shone. "That's enough. He's a good horse, and you take good care of him."

"I will, Jess."

They passed on down the land. Once, four miles onward, they started up a band of cattle. In that pale light, the large letter B upon these animals was clearly visible. A mossy-horned old bull took his position, dropped his head low, and gently rattled his horns at them.

They cut out around these animals still traveling northwest. Abruptly, Billy Ray said: "Look yonder, Jess. There's a light."

Jess looked and said mildly: "Sure is, isn't there." He adjusted their course toward some dark, bulky buildings that were dead ahead.

Billy Ray shot Jess a look. "You were coming here anyway," he said.

Jess chuckled. "The Lawtons live here. Their range adjoins the Big B."

They struck a flinty roadway and passed into the Lawton yard. Where that light burned was in the rear of the main house. Jess considered this as he moved forward. "Getting ready for bed," he told Billy Ray, and shot a gauging look at that sickle moon. "Kind of late at that." He drew up before a hitchrack in front of the house and sat undecided.

Billy Ray said: "Maybe we'd better not bother 'em."

From the onward verandah, something white rose up and seemed to float forward. Jess instantly got down, dropped his reins, and moved to meet this apparition.

"Margaret . . .?" he softly called.

The white silhouette froze. There was a long pause, then: "Jess? Is that you, Jess?"

Billy Ray watched from the saddle as those two moving blurs came together. His eyes grew big. Jess kissed this tall girl, and she clung to him, pressing her body into the curving full length of him, saying his name over and over.

Billy Ray was mightily embarrassed. He looked outward where there were other buildings. He considered the high sky, and he finally bent forward to run a small hand up Big Black's neck and mane.

The two shadows drew apart after a time and came down toward the hitchrack hand in hand. Billy Ray stole a secret look at the tall girl. She was sturdily made with slightly greater than average fullness at breast and hip, and her face, even in that weak light, was good to look at. She had a wide mouth with a heavy center fullness. Her eyes were misty now, but ordinarily, he thought, they would be smiling. She stopped beside Jess and smiled upward.

Jess said: "Billy Ray, this here is Margaret Lawton. Margaret, this is Billy Ray Patton."

The beautiful girl put forth her hand. Billy Ray shook it gravely, thankful for night's darkness, because he was furiously blushing. He could not recall ever before shaking hands with a woman. It left him feeling all prickly, as though with a heat rash, and he dropped Margaret Lawton's hand as quickly as he decently could. He felt tongue-tied, also, so when Margaret Lawton spoke, he had great difficulty speaking back.

"Would you like to get down," she asked, "and come up onto the porch, Billy Ray? I think there is some cake in the kitchen."

"No ma'am, but thank you," the boy managed. "I'll just stay here with Big Black . . . if you don't mind."

Jess put up a hand, squeezed Billy Ray's arm, and smiled. "I'd like to stay a little," he said. "Sure you wouldn't like to get down?"

Billy Ray shook his head at Jess. "I'll watch the horses," he murmured, and was greatly relieved when Jess and that beautiful girl moved off in the direction of the house.

It proved a long wait, but Billy Ray did not mind. He felt each small movement of the horse under him with pride. He sat on, his heart full, stroking the black horse's neck and shoulders, and when Jess finally came, it did not seem so long.

They rode from the Lawton yard side by side, neither speaking, but where the range began, again Jess said: "We could let 'em out a little." After he said this, they went down the night laughing back and forth.

It was, as near as Billy Ray could remember, the finest night of his life. When they slowed to come down across Big B's darkened yard, he tried hard to put these feelings into words.

They were dismounting when he said to Jess: "I wish . . ."

"Yes. What do you wish, Billy Ray?"

"Nothing. Jess? I'm not very good with words. But I know how I feel inside."

"Good?"

"I think I'm feeling better, Jess, but I'm really worried about Linda and my dad. But having Big Black now . . ."

Jess finished offsaddling. He turned the horses out and went back to throw an understanding arm around the boy's shoulders.

"I know," he softly said. "I was ten years old once. I know how a fellow can feel, sometimes."

They passed out of the barn and were headed to the bunkhouse when Jess sighted Dr. Hartman's top buggy yonder in front of the house. His arm dropped away from Billy Ray's shoulders. He walked on, saying nothing more until they were at the covered porch. Then he said: "You better get into bed, Billy Ray. Tomorrow's another day."

The lad twisted to look back. "Isn't that the buggy the doctor came here in, Jess?"

"Yes. But you trot along to bed. If there's worrying to be done, I'll do it for both of us."

"Maybe," murmured the boy, still solemnly eyeing that rig. "I ought to wake Pa up."

"No, let him sleep, son. If there's cause, I'll get him up. You head for the bunkhouse now, and get to sleep."

Billy Ray turned dutifully away and went shuffling outward over the yard. Jess waited a moment, then entered his house. He went quietly along to the lighted room where Linda Louise lay, eased open the door, and moved inside. His mother was there, hands clasped over her stomach. The doctor was at bedside, coat off and sleeves rolled up.

What stopped Jess in his tracks was the warmly steady look from a pair of liquid dark eyes in that huge bed. Linda Louise was gazing up at him with recognition. She made a tiny smile with her lips at Jess. He went forward and bent far down to hold her hand.

"Billy and I just went for a ride," he said gently. "In the moonlight. When you're up and around, all three of us will do that. Would you like that, Linda Louise?"

Her voice was faint and rough-sounding when she answered. "Yes, I'd like that. Why did you wait so long to come see me, Jess?"

Mary Bennett moved up closer, saying: "He's been in to see you, honey. But you've been asleep."

The doctor turned, put a somber gaze upon Jess, and jerked his head doorward. He did not speak.

Jess released Linda Louise's hand. "You get lots of rest," he said. "And I'll come back every day. Then, when you're ready, we'll go riding."

He left the room, waited in the hallway until his mother came out, and put a questioning look upon her. "What is it? My heart stopped when we rode in and saw Hartman's rig here this time of night."

His mother moved along toward the parlor as she spoke. "It was a routine call, he said, Jess. But he wanted to speak to you as soon as he got here. I think something is bothering him. I've known Jacob Hartman thirty years, son. I know when he's got something on his mind."

"It's not Linda Louise, then?"

"Not entirely."

Mary Bennett eased down into a chair. She ran a hand upward to smooth away a lock of hair. She smiled ruefully. "It's been a long time since I kept vigil over a sick child. I'd forgotten how it tires one."

"I'll get a woman from town," stated Jess.

His mother bristled. "You'll do no such thing. I'll have no strangers caring for that child."

Jess smiled. "You've known her exactly two days, and most of that time she's been unconscious or asleep."

"Ah, but a little girl and an old woman have many secrets in common, son." Mary's darkly ringed eyes shone over at Jess. "You never knew it, but I was disappointed when you were born. You were a boy, and I'd wanted a girl." Mary eased back in her chair. "You rode over to see Margaret," she said, making a statement of it. "I wondered when you'd get around to it."

"I took Billy Ray with me. On the way I gave him my black horse."

Mary Bennett inclined her head. "He needs a horse." She paused, then said: "Jacob had another reason for coming out here tonight, Jessie. He wanted another look at that man Patton. He had it, son. Did you know Samuel Patton was dying of lung fever?"

"Yes, he told me."

"Did he tell you how much time he has?"

"No. But I don't think he knows himself."

"Jacob says not more than six months, and probably much less than that."

Jess sat still.

Somewhere, beyond the house, a coyote made its wailing call in the faraway west. Moments later came an answering cry from the east.

Dr. Hartman came padding along into the parlor. He peered over at Jess, then at Mary Bennett, and began rolling down his sleeves. He did not offer to speak though until he was shrugging into a rusty and shapeless black coat. Then he said, in a voice sounding both tired and irritable: "The concussion was not as bad as I first thought. It's mending quite well. The broken leg seems to be coming along, too. About the chest . . . I'm not so sure. Actually, there are no broken ribs. It seems to be more a matter of deep contusions and bruises. Her breathing is shallow, which is to be expected. It does not sound thick . . . there is no accumulation of phlegm and no bubbling." The doctor went to a chair and threw himself into it. He stared a moment at the empty, black old fireplace. "If she catches a cold, it will probably be fatal."

He looked up at Jess then over to Mary. "But in the middle of a scorching summer, who catches colds? Still, be sure she is not in a draft. Otherwise, I think she might make it. She's a strong child and very healthy. Those are the things one needs . . . strength and robust health."

The doctor let his voice drift off into a deep silence. He ran a hand over his face. "I'm tired," he said, after a while. "I'm tired to the soul of my body."

"I'll make some coffee," said Mary, and would have arisen but the medical man waved a hand at her.

"It's not that kind of weariness, Mary. It's a bowing down of the spirit. It's a losing of faith in humankind. Coffee won't help, nor will whiskey."

Mary, seeing how slumped the doctor sat, said: "Jacob, you need rest. It might not even hurt if you saw a doctor yourself. You looked gray when you drove in here this evening."

"I am gray," muttered Hartman. He got up out of the chair and paced forward toward the front window. With both hands clasped behind his back, he said: "Jess, did your mother tell you how long Samuel Patton has left of his life?"

"She told me, yes."

"Then I only have one more unpleasant duty left," said the doctor, turning fully around and staring over at Jess. "Mike Slattery shot and killed Sheriff Blaine Richards this afternoon."

CHAPTER EIGHT

Jess rode alone into the town of Hereford the following morning early. He passed down Absaroka Valley in pale new-day light encountering no one until, upon the outskirts of town, he met a brace of horsemen who, upon seeing him and recognizing him, drew up to wait his approach.

One of these riders was aged Clem Brite of the Ox-Yoke cow outfit. The other was dark and swarthy Hugh Shannon. Old Brite put a knowing look upon Jess and said: "Good morning. I reckon you heard, too."

"I heard," said Jess, and looked past Brite to Hugh Shannon. "How did it happen?"

"No one knows, exactly. Blaine had a warrant for Mike for hitting that camp and injuring the little girl. He rode out to Slattery's Circle S to serve it. Couple hours later a brace of riders came to the edge of town with Blaine tied facedown across his saddle. They hoorahed the horse on into town but didn't come in themselves. Then they turned tail and left."

Jess looked from Clem Brite back to Shannon. He said: "Doc Hartman said Mike shot Blaine."

Shannon shrugged. "We all figure that's about the size of it, Jess. Mike's been hiring gunslingers for over a month. In fact, there are a couple of new ones in town right now at the hotel, waiting for Mike to come get them."

"How do you know that?"

"Hell, I talked to 'em less than a half hour ago. They're Arizona boys. They said Slattery sent for them."

"But I don't understand this!" exclaimed Jess, making a deep frown. "What's he doing this for? Blaine told me yesterday he'd just about rid the valley of squatters. So why is Mike hiring gunmen?"

Old Clem Brite turned his head, spat, and turned it back. "All the squatters aren't gone yet," he said dryly. "There is a batch of 'em camped over near Castle Rock, at the spring."

Jess, knowing this place Brite was speaking of was well within the confines of Slattery's deeded range, said: "Does Mike know that?"

"He must," said Shannon. "That's why we're in town this morning. Someone's got to be appointed sheriff to take Blaine's place. Then, whoever that man is, he's got to get out there and stop murder from being done."

Both the cowmen were looking straight at Jess. He returned that regard with a dawning realization. "Oh no!" he exclaimed stoutly. "Not me, fellows. I don't know the first thing about law enforcement."

"You don't have to," retorted old Brite. "All you got to know is how to lead us and salt Mike Slattery down. The law books can go hang."

Jess was adamant. "Not on your damned lives!" he exclaimed. "I'll go with you . . . but not as any kind of a lawman."

Brite and Shannon exchanged a long look, then Brite said very seriously: "Jess, if Slattery ain't stopped right now, he's going to involve us all in a real shooting war. Let him kill a few tomfool squatters and the gov'nor'll send on the militia, there'll be Federal lawmen swarming in here, and, unless I miss my guess, all the empty-pocketed gunslicks in the West will be riding in to hire out their guns to us or the other side. Boy, I've seen this happen before, and it always starts with just a couple of killings."

"I'm not arguing that," stated Jess. "All I'm saying is that . . ."

"You won't lead us," interrupted the old man acidly, and accompanied this with a strong headshake. "Then suggest someone who will."

Jess looked straight at Brite. "You," he said.

Brite snorted. "I'm sixty-eight years old. How long would I last, playing a young man's game?"

"Then let Hugh do it."

But Shannon's answer to that was a death knell. "The others wouldn't follow me, Jess. You know that. I'm not a big cowman. Besides, I don't have the respect you have among the ranchers."

Jess named several other cowmen. Brite and Shannon had solid objections to each of them. Then Shannon said: "Jess, while we're arguin' here in the road, Slattery's probably ridin'."

Jess took back a deep breath. "What do we need a lawman along for anyway?" he asked. "Clem, you go on into town, round up a posse, and have someone sworn in to take Blaine's place if you're of a mind to. Then hightail it for Castle Rock. Hugh and I'll go on from here."

Clem peered at both young men. "Just the pair of you?" he asked, looking and sounding uncertain about this. "Jess, like we told you, Mike's got hired gunmen. At least seven of them. If the brace o' you go riding into Circle S's yard rattling your horns, you'll go up in smoke."

"We won't head for Circle S," stated Jess, turning his horse. "We'll be at Castle Rock."

Brite was skeptical of this, too. "Slattery's been saying you're siding with squatters. Now he'll be able to prove it."

"Look, Clem, just get that posse and make a run for the spring. What Slattery thinks no longer matters. If this thing's as bad you say, then how we stop it is not important . . . only *that* we stop it matters. Hugh, are you with me?"

"To the hilt," snapped Shannon, and booted out his horse.

Clem Brite yelled after them: "Be careful! Mike'll likely have scouts out to intercept anyone heading for Castle Rock."

It being doubtful whether the two loping riders heard this, Brite yanked his own animal around, hung in the hooks, and made a dash for the center of Hereford.

* * * * *

The ride to Castle Rock was no little jaunt. Where Absaroka Valley's northernmost buttressing mountains came ramming down hard upon the plain, east of that descending trail Jess had recently come over with the Pattons, stood forth a towering great monolith. It was anchored to the upper mountainside and had a prominent outthrust that shaded a thick aspen grove down lower. This was called Castle Rock because of the way it stood out from the rest of the mountainside with its fluting spires and rough ramparts.

Here, against the flank of those abrupt hills, was the northernmost limit of Absaroka Valley. Here also was the boundary line of Mike Slattery's Circle S range. In the aspen grove was the spring Clem Brite had mentioned. It was a favorite watering place for animals, wild and tame, in summertime, for the water came boiling up from a deep underground cavern and was both sweet and cold.

Many years earlier when the Indians had roamed this land, Castle Rock Spring had been a prominent rendezvous spot. There remained considerable evidence of their long association with this place, not only in the age-old and layers-deep smoke smudges rising straight up the mountain's face, but also in among the tumbled boulders where artists in eons gone had laboriously etched and colored elaborate pictographs.

But in order for Jess and Hugh Shannon to reach the spring, they had to pass over most of Mike Slattery's southerly and, eventually, his northward range. This knowledge had been what had prompted old Clem Brite to shout his warning.

Still, since both Jess and Hugh were quite familiar with the land, they knew this, too. They therefore rode northeastward with their heads up, their eyes constantly moving, and their hands never distant from gun butts. They passed swiftly along, utilizing each shadowed arroyo, each stand of trees, every ruse they knew, to go undetected.

Once, when they paused in behind a little knoll to rest their animals, they sighted a string of horsemen riding southward in a dusty run. Jess watched these men for some time, trying to imagine their purpose. Southward, in the direction of those horsemen, but beyond sight, lay Slattery's home ranch.

Hugh Shannon, his Indian eyes narrowed ahead, said: "I think our squatters have just been discovered."

Jess had come to this conclusion also, but what he said was: "Why didn't they attack them, then?"

"Riding back to alert Mike and get the rest of the Circle S crew, more than likely."

"There are seven of them, Hugh. If they didn't dare attack, I'm beginning to wonder how many of those squatters are at the spring."

"Must be a bunch of 'em," said Shannon, easing his horse forward.

They went hurrying along for another mile, or until Castle Rock's great prominence stood out clearly in the warming early morning, with fierce sunlight glittering across it, making a dull, hot fire. Then they saw three riders poking leisurely along at the base of the mountains, traveling due east, and stopped this time in a plum thicket near a waterway to observe these strangers.

It was not difficult in the clear brightness to see that these were not cattlemen. Their horses looked more accustomed to collars than saddles. They walked along with a feather-legged plodding gait. The men upon their backs were roughly dressed, carried rifles instead of saddle carbines, and one of them had a barren blue doe tied aft of his saddle.

"Been meat hunting," mused Shannon. "Must've been up in the hills, otherwise we'd have heard the shot."

"If they were," reasoned Jess, watching those moving men, "then they undoubtedly saw Slattery's gunmen."

Hugh frowned and scratched his jaw. "They sure don't act alarmed," he said. "If I'd seen seven gunmen, I think I'd be a little worried."

Jess shrugged. Perhaps the onward men, obviously members of some squatter camp, had seen Slattery's men but had attached no significance to them. He sat on in silence waiting until the horsemen had faded out where the cliff gloom was deepest, then rode at a walk to a nearby land swell.

Here, with Hugh beside him, he rode up, topped out, and halted. From this little eminence, he had a good long view of the onward country.

"There," said Shannon, sounding triumphant. "There's smoke rising right straight up from deep in the aspens."

"Breakfast fire," stated Jess, and swore a mild oath. "They sure don't care who sees them."

"Maybe they're newcomers. Maybe they come down from that

old road through the mountains to the north and don't know what kind of trouble they're in."

Jess, straining to see movement in among the yonder aspen trees, had another notion concerning the carelessness of these illegal land-grabbers. "Or maybe," he told Hugh, "there are enough of them to put up a good scrap and they know it."

They rode onward, and since there was no practical route to the aspen grove that would adequately hide their coming, except along the base of the mountain, they rode slowly. In this manner Jess thought it unlikely they would be shot at, at least until they were given a chance to state their business. He was right. But what he had no idea about at all was that their entire approach for that final two miles had been observed by overhead sentries. That their route and actions had been carefully sent down to the squatter camp, and that now, as they passed slowly along through cliff shadows, unkempt, cold-eyed men were taking up guns and moving leisurely down to meet them where the trees stood, and where filigreed patterns of shade mottled each of these raffish people so that even the careful eyes of Hugh Shannon saw nothing, not even after they had ridden past the first squatters and were into the first tier of aspens. Then a premonition sang out along Jess's nerves, causing him to draw rein and look over at Hugh.

"This is too easy," he softly said. "Slattery'll cut them to pieces."

A drawling-soft voice behind them said in response to this: "Well, that there cutting works both ways, boys."

Jess saw Shannon's eyes widen in surprise. They both twisted in their saddles to look around.

Four men stood there. Each of them had a long-barreled rifle with a maple stock—these were fragile-seeming weapons. The men also wore belted pistols, but they stood now cradling those long rifles and seemed, in their quiet stances, to be relying upon the rifles, not their pistols.

They were rough-looking men, tall, angular, rawboned, and three of them were fully bearded. Two of them chewed tobacco with a rhythmic, steady cadence, their eyes fixed steadily forward in expressions of absolute confidence, absolute calm fearlessness.

The attire of the people was nondescript. Their hats were shapeless, their boots were low-heeled with their trousers stuffed inside them freighter fashion. They had nothing in common with cowmen, so far as Jess could see, but their fearlessness impressed him. He could not imagine these men doing anything impetuously. Now, clearly prepared for trouble, they stood easy, loosely assessing the pair of armed, mounted men in front of them.

"More," murmured Hugh.

Jess gradually swung his head. Other men of this same bizarre type were soundlessly moving forward upon them from among the trees. He counted eleven of them, all carrying those delicate-appearing long rifles.

That bearded older man who had spoken now walked quietly around in front of Jess. He spat dark liquid, ran a hand over chin whiskers, and skewered Jess with his very pale, very capable eyes.

"Who is this Slattery you said was fixin' to cut us to pieces?" he asked, in a voice both drawlingly soft and at the same time piercingly nasal.

"He owns the land you're squatting on," stated Jess. "He owns Circle S Ranch."

"Then," reasoned this lanky mountaineer, "them fellers we seen hustlin' on southward a while ago must've been his hirelings. You reckon that's so, stranger?"

"That's so," answered Jess. "They are hired gunmen . . . professional man-killers."

"I see. Well, we're obliged to you-all for comin' on to warn us." Those calm, steady eyes became ironic now. "That is what you boys come up here to do, ain't it? We'd plumb hate to figure you was some of Mistah Slattery's professional man-killers, too."

Hugh's lips lifted slightly in a hard little grin. He looked over at Jess and gently wagged his head with clear meaning. He'd never before encountered people like these, but he definitely admired their fearlessness.

Jess replied to the mountaineer, saying: "That's partly why we're here, yes. The other part is to ask you to move on."

The lanky man shifted the hold on his rifle. He looked slowly around at his companions. Then he said: "Tell you what, boys . . . come along and break a little bread with us'ns, an' we'll sort of de-scuss this matter."

Jess smiled in spite of himself. "All right," he replied, and got down to stand beside his horse.

Hugh also dismounted. He stood for a moment before saying to the lanky man: "Are we guests or prisoners?"

A mountaineer walked up close to Hugh and peered intently at him. "That's plumb up to you-all," he stated. "But if you got notions 'bout usin' them guns . . ." The man shifted back a step, raising his eyes to the overhead cliff face. "Look yonder," he murmured.

Jess and Hugh looked upward. Where a stone ledge ran along beneath Castle Rock's thrusting lip lay four motionless men with four of those long-barreled rifles pointing downward in dazzling, bright sunlight.

CHAPTER NINE

The squatter camp was deep in the aspen grove at Castle Rock Spring. There were five wagons which, in Jess's appraising eyes, were no better than the wagon Samuel Patton had also driven into the valley. The people themselves were courteous and observing and taciturn. They gravely served Jess and Hugh Shannon fried meat upon tin plates, and coffee strong enough to float a horseshoe, from their communal cooking fire, then the womenfolk faded back, leaving the men to squat there in mellow shade, eating and conversing.

The bearded older man who had first addressed them appeared to be nominal spokesmen for these prairie gypsies. He told Jess his name was Tolivar—Moses Tolivar—that two-thirds of the others were also named Tolivar, and that, besides being "kin folks one t' the otherns" they had come from Tennessee originally, had crossed the Missouri near Independence, Missouri, and had been following the buffalo herds as hunters for six years, but now, with the "buffler" gone, they had decided to locate a good mountain meadow and settle down.

Jess told them Absaroka Valley had no free land. To this Moses Tolivar said easily: "If a feller squats and puts up buildings and fences in . . . then all he's got to do is pay taxes fer three y'ars, and the land is his'n. That's the law, young feller."

Hugh finished eating, put aside his plate, raised a tin coffee cup, and said to Tolivar over the cup's dented rim: "You'd never get it done, law or no law. There are too many cattlemen in here, Mr. Tolivar. They'd burn you out and bury those that resisted."

Tolivar considered Shannon's swarthy countenance a moment before speaking again. "You 'pear to be part Injun to me, young feller, and I allow Injuns'd know how folks take land from one another by force. Well, sir, all we want is a place to settle our bodies and maybe, later on, plant our bones. The Injuns owned all this country once . . . then come the whites and took it from 'em. That don't make what the whites done right. But that's how it works, an' we figure to do the same thing." Tolivar parted his beard and deftly spat through it. "As for buryin' folks, mistah . . . we know a right smart about that, too."

Jess gazed at the roundabout faces. There was not a man in his view who did not look willing and able to take care of himself. He began to wish he and Hugh hadn't come here; to wish they'd left these people and Mike Slattery to fight it out. But he had never before met any squatters and had hazily thought they would be people like the Pattons—helpless in the face of cowmen wrath.

"How 'bout you, son?" Tolivar said, addressing Jess. "You feel like your friend here?"

Jess tried to catch his thoughts, to pin them down. He spoke slowly when he ultimately answered. "To some extent, yes, Mr. Tolivar. You have about twenty men. I'm not doubting at all that they are capable men. But Mike Slattery has at least fifteen, and ten of those are professional gunmen. On top of that, even if you whipped Slattery, the other cowmen would fight you, too. They own their land. It's patented. There's no free graze or homestead land in this valley. I know how you feel about wanting a place to raise your kids and build your houses and graze your critters. My grandfather felt the same way when he trailed the first herd into the Absaroka country. But between then and now has passed a lot of time. You can't preempt land any more, and if you try it here and now, Mr. Tolivar, a lot of men are going to get killed."

Old Tolivar kept his pale gaze upon Jess for a long time. Then he sighed and looked around at the men of his camp. They were, for the most part, quietly impassive. Jess thought they were carefully considering what he had just said. He got the impression that these people were fair and honest but as poor as people could be and therefore willing to run risks.

"He talks straight out," said Tolivar to his companions. "This boy's got no forked tongue."

Hugh Shannon looked long at old Tolivar after he said this. "That's Injun talk," he murmured.

Tolivar nodded. "We been among 'em," he stated. "We wintered with the red folks. You see, boy, we got a lot in common with Injuns. We ain't 'zactly welcome on the land either, although our granddaddies give their blood to make it all one country."

Jess shot a speculating look skyward where the faded, brassy sky held that fierce yellow disc. "They've had time to get to Slattery' and partway back," he said, referring to those seven riders they had earlier observed. "Whatever we're going to accomplish here, we'd better do quickly."

Shannon was pensively studying Tolivar. "I don't want to fight you," he said quietly, "but I own land here, too. So does Jess. In fact his Big B is the richest ranch in our valley. Why don't you save us all a heap of grief, mister. Just load up and head on down the valley. Beyond the mountains southward, there is more land. There's a prairie down there that runs for five hundred miles. There's enough free graze and water and good land down there for the lot of you to stake out homesteads."

"We come from the north," stated a mountaineer. "We got no way of knowin' about this other place you're speakin' of, friend."

Jess, sensing this man's mild doubt, said: "It's true enough. In fact we'll guide you there."

Old Tolivar said from an impassive face: "That's right neighborly of you."

Jess looked up at the bearded older man. "I'm not offering out of friendship. We'll have to go with you if you go south, because you'll be crossing the full length of our valley and the way folks feel right now about squatters there would be serious trouble unless some of us were along with you."

Tolivar inclined his patriarchal head at this. He then refilled Jess's coffee cup and was bending to do the same for Hugh Shannon, when a thin, musical call came from up the rearward mountainside. Tolivar's arm stopped moving. He swung his head.

The mountaineers around Jess and Hugh Shannon rose up off the ground, took their rifles in hand, and stood easy, waiting for Moses Tolivar to arise also.

"I reckon this must be your friend Slattery," said the bearded old man, getting upright and reaching for the handsomely engraved gun at his side. "Don't figure we got much choice now, boys, 'ceptin' to carve our mark on those there professional man-killers you warned us of."

As Jess and Hugh sprang up, the mountaineers began silently drifting off through the aspens. Old Tolivar was the last to turn.

With a mild expression, he said: "You fellers can likely still ride clear if you start right now and ride right smart toward the west. If they give you any trouble, we'll divert 'em with a little musket fire." Tolivar pushed out a gnarled hand. "We're beholden to you for warnin' us, an' maybe, if God is plumb willin', we'll cross trails again, one day."

Jess said sharply: "Hold on! We can't get away now, and I'm not sure we want to anyway. But before you open up on Slattery, let's try to settle this thing without a battle."

Tolivar nodded gravely. "Sure enough," he drawled. "We never fire the first shot, son. It's against our principles to do that." He looked steadily at Jess. "You two want to ride out and palaver?"

Jess nodded, looking at Hugh for confirmation. Shannon nodded, too, but he seemed glum at the prospect of facing Slattery's gun crew.

"They mightn't let you," Tolivar stated. Then he hoisted his rifle into the crook of one arm and smiled without humor. "But you go try anyway. If they cut you down, I promise . . . I give you my word . . . they'll fall right beside you."

Jess and Hugh went along through the trees with Moses Tolivar. They passed kneeling mountaineers who were checking shot pouches, scalping knives, and cocking mechanisms.

Hugh said in a low whisper at Jess's side: "These people have been through this a hundred times before. I got a bad feeling for Slattery, Jess . . . and I feel good about that, damn him."

Where the aspen grove dwindled and the onward land began, Jess moved clear of Tolivar, going toward his horse. Hugh Shannon stood a long time, gazing about him. Then, with a hard head wag, he swung up into his saddle and looked at Jess.

Onward, fanned out across the land under that pitiless sun, was a thin long line of armed riders. Jess gazed from north to south until he saw the big, reddish bulk of Mike Slattery. Bitterness welled up in him. Blaine Richards had been a good friend. Linda Louise was lying broken and half-dead because of that approaching horseman.

Jess's expression was bleak as he let those riders come on. Then a big hand fell lightly upon his knee, and from the ground Moses Tolivar said: "I passed the word, son. First one o' them as touches his gun is a dead man." The hand fell away. "The Injuns got a sayin'." He looked round at dark Hugh Shannon also sitting there waiting. "They say . . . 'Brave up, brave up. This is a good day to die.'"

Tolivar looked out where that line of horsemen was drawing down to a halt beyond carbine range. He smiled and softly said: "Mistah Slattery miscalculates. Sure 'nough a carbine won't reach him out there. But our rifles'll shoot another hundred yards beyond him, then pick up stones and pelt his backsides, too." He nodded to Jess. "Good luck, son. If you come back, we'll talk some more 'bout that other land farther south."

Jess eased off his reins. At his side Hugh Shannon drew back a loud breath and also passed on out of the aspen grove.

One of Mike Slattery's riders instantly spied those two slow-pacing riders and let off a high cry.

At Jess's side, Shannon said: "From the fry pan into the fire." He was anticipating a shot, but none came. Then, a hundred yards farther on, he spoke to Jess again: "They won't let us ride back."

"If we can stall long enough," mumbled Jess, "we won't have to ride back. Clem ought to have his posse in the saddle by now. Even a madman like Slattery isn't crazy enough to fight someone in front of him and in back of him, too."

"That," stated Shannon firmly, "is something I wouldn't want to bet a penny on."

Those onward horsemen were sitting their mounts like graven images, without a sound or a movement. Not until Jess and Hugh were a goodly distance from the aspens did one of those riders urge his animal onward to meet them. Then, in response to a sharp order from this man, two other horsemen also eased out, but these two remained well behind and off on each side of that foremost rider.

"Slattery!" exclaimed Shannon dryly to Jess. "He's as erect on that saddle as though he's got a ramrod down his back."

Jess could sense Slattery's hostility while a hundred yards still separated them. "He's going to start that talk about me being on the side of the squatters," he murmured to Hugh, without once taking his eyes off the Circle S owner.

Behind them was total stillness. Onward, where those Circle S men sat still and watching, was also a deep stillness.

Overhead, the midmorning sun punished earth and men and animals with its constant burning. There was not a cloud anywhere in the heavens, and where heat struck hard upon that northward cliff face of miles-deep granite, the waves of heat rolled outward, layer after layer of it. Sweat came easily to men and horses under these circumstances.

Jess swung his head to rid himself of this oily wetness.

Sunlight glinted wickedly from naked carbines athwart men's laps dead ahead and off rein chains and silvered bits as well. The sound of horses moving over stony earth seemed loud to Jess, as did the abrasive chukkering sounds made by rubbing saddle leather. Then he could see Mike Slattery's red-raw face beneath its shading hat brim and the wrath encompassed there was so powerful he had to brace into it.

It was now no longer possible to speak aside to Hugh Shannon without Slattery and his bodyguard hearing what was said. He wished he'd worked out some strategy with Hugh, for he was now convinced that not only would Slattery block any attempt on their part to return to the aspen grove but that he intended to have them both shot down as well.

CHAPTER TEN

"I wish," said Slattery when Jess was close, "the other ranchers could see you now, ridin' out of that squatter camp."

Jess made no reply. He reined up, as did Hugh Shannon.

Slattery put his sulfur gaze upon Shannon. His mouth curved in scorn.

"You too?" he said.

"Yeah," Shannon snarled back. "And with good reason. We came here to avoid trouble if we could. To get those folks to move on."

Slattery said a savage word, then returned his glare to Jess. "You can't avoid trouble . . . either of you. Neither can those damned squatters. Look behind me. There are enough guns back there to clean you two out, and that nest of scum, too."

"I wouldn't bet on that," said Jess. "And if you're smart you won't push it, Mike. There are close to twenty mountaineers in that aspen grove, all armed and waiting."

Slattery contemptuously shot an onward glance toward the squatter camp. "Fifty," he ultimately said, "and I'd still ride over 'em."

"I don't think so," muttered Hugh Shannon. "These aren't the same breed of cats as most squatters, Mike."

Slattery swung his gaze back. "You've turned squatter lover too, I see," he said to Shannon. "Well, you backed the wrong horse, Hugh. You'll live to regret it."

"Like Blaine Richards lived to regret it?" asked Jess. "Mike, I'll ask you for the last time . . . back off. You're in enough trouble as it is. Killing squatters here at Castle Rock isn't going to do you any good at all."

Slattery's fierce gaze burned against Jess. "Blaine Richards had that comin'. He's been getting' between me and squatters for a long time. No man, not even you, Jess Bennett, crosses me andlives."

Jess twisted to put a resigned look upon Hugh. Shannon saw and understood this look, and he shrugged at Mike Slattery without speaking but with unmistakable meaning. Whatever ensued next was squarely upon Slattery's shoulders.

Slattery viewed those two in front of him for a halting moment, then he raised a hand. Instantly, one of those riders back a ways kneed his animal forward. The other rider did not move, but he did drop a hand casually to his hip holster and keep his eyes fully forward.

"I'll give you both a chance," said Mike Slattery, his face smoothing out, becoming still and inward. "Two to two. You and Hugh against me an' Asa here."

Jess looked at the rider called Asa. He became sardonic. He had never before seen this other man, but he'd seen a dozen just like him. Gunman. His profession was obvious in each move the stranger made after he halted his animal some six or eight feet from Slattery. He was a hawk-faced, thin-featured man with small round eyes that scarcely blinked. He sat easy now, on his horse, watching

Jess and Hugh. He had recently removed a pair of gloves that now hung from his belt.

Mike Slattery looked triumphantly at Jess. He was savoring this moment. He was near to smiling.

"Big B," he said softly, contemptuously. "The biggest cow outfit in the valley. I wonder who'll run it after you're gone? I wonder how cheap a man could buy the Big B range, then, Jess? You Bennetts had it all your way in Absaroka Valley long enough. Three generations. Now it's someone else's turn."

Jess, with a dawning notion, looked hard at Slattery. He said, in a gradually firming-up tone: "Mike, it isn't the squatters, really, is it? It never was. It's the rest of us here in the valley . . . and it's your greed. You just used the squatters to bring this other thing on. Isn't that it?"

Slattery, swollen with his coming victory, said: "You're a fool, Jess. A damned fool. Anyone else would have figured the answer to that a long time ago." He paused to shoot a glance over at Hugh Shannon. "You're on the wrong side. I told you that, Hugh. If you'd played along with me, you'd have lived to get some Big B land. Now, you'll go out with Jess."

Shannon sat mutely, staring at red-faced big Mike Slattery. The byplay between Mike and Jess was just beginning to make sense to him.

"I'll be damned," he softly said, after a time, and looked at the motionless, expressionless gunman at Slattery's side. "Mister," he said to this man, "if you kill one of us, you'll never get out of this valley alive. By now everyone knows what happened to Sheriff Richards. The cowmen'll be gatherin'. There's a posse on its way up here right now. You better think it over."

Asa sat there like stone, his eyes steady, his lips tightly locked, and his body balancing between drawing and waiting.

Slattery said: "Pray, you two!" Then he let his right shoulder down a little, let his arms turn loose and his eyes draw out narrow.

A little puff of soiled smoke came from the aspen grove, followed by a sharp report. Asa's mouth flew open, his body jerked, and his eyes went awry. He fell sideways from the saddle, making a sodden sound when he struck earth. He did not move again.

Mike Slattery's head jerked around. He stared with color draining out of his florid face. Then he stiffened forward as Jess said: "Easy, Mike, don't make a move."

Jess had his gun barrel lying even with a saddle swell sighted in upon Slattery's belt buckle. He had taken full advantage of the diversion to accomplish this.

"I tried to warn you, Mike. Hugh tried to tell you also . . . Those people aren't the kind of squatters you're used to chousing."

Slattery looked over Jess's shoulder where that little dirty puff of gun smoke was drifting straight up in the breathless day. The distance was great, and this was what troubled him now. He put another gauging look down at Asa, then over to the aspen grove again.

"Luck," he muttered. "A lucky shot."

Hugh Shannon had his right hand upon his gun. He had not drawn, and now it appeared that he would not. He said to Slattery: "Fill your hand and find out whether it was lucky shootin' or not."

Slattery did not move. He just continued to stare at the aspen grove. He was turning something over in his mind. After a time he said to Jess: "If that's how your squatter friends want it, that's how it'll be." He snugged back his reins, spun his horse, and went stiffly trotting back toward his riders.

Jess put up his gun. He felt very alone, out there between two armed camps with no cover closer than the aspen grove.

"Let's go back," he said to Hugh. "Maybe we won't make it, but we've got to try."

They turned, started riding back, but did this at a walk. Once, Jess turned to see what Slattery was doing. He glimpsed a horseman dismounting near where Slattery stood, obviously having been ordered to do this. The horseman put up his carbine, aiming where Jess and Hugh rode along. Sunlight danced along that distant barrel.

Jess opened his mouth to cry a warning to Hugh, when onward, dead ahead, came another sharp slamming rifle report. The distance here was well over a thousand yards. Slattery's man sprang high into the air, flung away his carbine, and went over backward to land in a broken heap.

Hugh Shannon jerked upright at that shot and afterward roweled his animal, breaking over into a fierce run for the grove. Jess ran along with him. Hugh was twisting to see behind them.

Slattery's riders, astonished by the range of that killing shot, were breaking away in all directions, running hard to get beyond rifle range. Their cries of alarm, of amazement, came thinly through the air.

Jess made it into the trees and flung out of the saddle. Hugh was right behind him.

Moses Tolivar came forward with a wiping stick in one hand and his fired long rifle in the other hand. His face was grave but his eyes glinted pleasantly.

"Some folks got to be showed," he drawled to Jess. "That second one was fixin' to shoot you in the back. Us folks don't hold with that kind o' fightin'. Feller wants to fight, he ought to be decent 'nough to face his enemy."

A bracketing sound of faraway gunfire erupted. Jess stepped clear of the trees to consider this. Slattery's riders were shooting toward the grove but aiming well above it in the hope of dropping bullets upon their enemies. He paced back into the tree shade without commenting on this senseless shooting. A number of the mountaineers, also turning their backs on this kind of fighting in deep and quiet scorn, crowded up around Jess and Hugh Shannon. One of them spat aside, swiped the back of a big hand over his lips.

Finally, he said: "Jumped the gun a mite on that first feller. But a feller dasn't wait too long with them pistol men. They can draw right fast once they commence movin'. A feller can't take the chance." He smiled apologetically at Jess and shuffled off toward camp.

Others went along with him, all silent, all thoughtfully moving along with calm deliberateness.

Tolivar stroked his shaggy beard, all the time eyeing Jess. "Well now, son, you tried," he said placatingly, "can't no man do more. We allow as how a man can't never command success . . . he can only deserve it."

Tolivar peered through the trees out where Slattery's horsemen were coming all together. He said next: "What you reckon they'll figure to do now?"

Jess was wondering about Clem Brite's posse. He thought they'd had ample time to get up here by now. But he said nothing of these men.

"Wait until dark, Mr. Tolivar, then slip up close in the dark and try to fire your camp."

Tolivar nodded over this. "Sure 'nough," he drawled. "When things are burnin' bright, they'll have light to shoot us by." He turned away from watching Slattery. "It's the old Injun way of doin'. Well, we seen our share o' that kind o' fightin', too."

Hugh Shannon now said, with a quick ring to his voice: "Riders, Jess. Far back down the valley. Looks from the dust like a big party of them."

Jess turned. He saw the approaching dust, but he also noticed that Slattery's men were beating along eastward in a steady lope, leaving the area. "Slattery's seen that dust as well," he said. "Let's get mounted, Hugh."

As they swung up, Tolivar, after squinting a long time at that dust, hoisted his rifle to the crook of one arm, saying: "Bring your friends to camp, boys. I'll step along and have enough water added to the stew to accommodate 'em."

They watched the old man walk away, then rode out into that smashing heat again. Only now Hugh Shannon was smiling. A hundred yards farther along, he laughed aloud. When Jess turned, Hugh said, slapping his thigh: "Those are the doggonedest people I ever saw in my life."

Jess also smiled. "That's what the Mexicans thought at the Alamo down in Texas. It was the same breed of Tennesseans who killed near two thousand of 'em down there without losing a man for thirteen days."

Hugh sobered. He rode along watching two different dust banners, one retreating swiftly southeastward, the other coming steadily on from the direction of Hereford.

When Jess was certain Shannon was thinking only of that oncoming relief, Shannon said abruptly: "Jess, I got to have one of those long rifles, no matter what it costs."

"I reckon Slattery feels the same way. Come on, I recognize Clem's grulla horse."

* * * * *

They met the posse a long mile southward and let it come into the minimal shade of a land swell to them.

Old Clem Brite was profusely sweating, as were most of the twenty-five riders with him. Brite looked dour, and when Jess smiled at the nickel badge upon the older man's shirt, Brite snapped: "Well, someone had to make this confounded business legal-like. No one else would put the thing on." Brite looked off toward the east. "We saw dust on our way up here," he said, then waited.

Jess related what had occurred. The possemen, mostly townsmen from Hereford, crowded up to listen. When Jess told of the two killings, old Clem squinted a doubting look at him.

"How far did you say?" he asked.

Hugh answered: "A thousand yards at least, Clem."

"Pshaw! You know better'n that, Hugh."

"It's true," said Jess, lifting his rein hand. "Come on, and see for yourself."

They rode back to where the second gunman had been shot. He was no longer there, having been carried off by Slattery's crew, but there was drying blood upon the grass to show where he'd fallen.

The possemen dismounted, flocked around old Clem, then did exactly as Brite did. They raised their heads to estimate the distance of that shot. Afterward, they muttered among themselves, and when Jess led them along to where the rider called Asa had also been shot, they let their wondering talk dwindle into strong and speculative silence.

Clem Brite said: "Let's go up to that camp, Jess. It's been thirty years since I've seen a Pennsylvania rifle. Since repeaters come out, those old muzzle-loaders have become as scarce as hen's teeth."

Hugh Shannon rode along in the midst of that strongly armed body of men, listening to the talk. When Clem's words ended, he said, with feeling: "There isn't a Winchester carbine made that can match those long rifles for accuracy. Clem, you wouldn't have believed that shootin' unless you'd seen it."

Brite put a tolerant gaze upon the younger man. He seemed on the verge of replying to this, but in the end he didn't. He only let a little knowing smile pass fleetingly across his face.

They were still a hundred yards off when quietly moving men began filtering out of the aspen grove. Foremost among them was old Moses Tolivar, rifle riding loosely in the crook of one arm, his streaked great beard reflecting hot sunlight in a rusty way.

"I'll be damned," someone muttered. "Looks like a character straight out of history."

Tolivar raised his arm in greeting. Jess and Clem Brite returned this salutation.

CHAPTER ELEVEN

The squatters were silent in the face of the Hereford posse's approach, and afterward, when the townsmen and ranchers were led along by Tolivar to their camp, these taciturn people listened and observed but were unobtrusive. Handsome tall girls and sturdy women served up a meal of venison stew and black coffee. The possemen were impressed by the grave bearing of these people and by old Tolivar's drawling recitation of their endless travels. At Clem Brite's request one of the long rifles was brought forth to be inspected.

Jess glimpsed children lying beneath wagons, watching the newcomers with round eyes. He also saw Hugh Shannon put a long, long look upon a tall, willowy girl with auburn hair and jet-black eyes as she passed among the men with a huge granite-ware coffeepot.

He was listening to Brite and Moses Tolivar discussing comparative merits of guns when a lanky man stepped into camp from the aspen grove, saying: "There's a rider comin' on like Old Nick was after him, Mose."

Tolivar at once arose. All the other men got up quickly, too, reaching for weapons and looking uncertainly at Clem Brite and Tolivar.

Jess said: "If he's alone he can't be planning trouble." Then he turned to walk back through the trees where he could see this newcomer.

"It's John Burr," he said aloud, and at once a coldness touched down through him.

"I never saw him ride like that before!" exclaimed Hugh Shannon. Then, struck with the same premonition that had come to Jess, Hugh ran after Jess out through the trees onto the plain.

The Big B's foreman yanked down to a sliding halt and yelled from the saddle at sight of Jess: "Slattery's crew hit the ranch, Jess! They shot the place up pretty bad. Doc Hartman was there . . . he stopped a slug. So did Slim Perkins, who was ridin' to the home ranch from a line camp and got caught between the yard and Slattery's men."

"Go on back!" shouted Jess. "I'll get my horse and be right with you."

As he wheeled about, Hugh Shannon went hurriedly back with him. They got astride and Jess, ignoring the cries of Clem Brite's possemen, spun out of the grove in a belly-down run. A hundred feet behind him, Hugh Shannon called down as he too went forward: "Clem, you better come!"

* * * * *

Jess dared not push his horse in that killing midday heat, but he alternated between a loose lope and a standing trot. He and Hugh left John Burr far back. Burr's horse had been ridden too hard already. He had to be content to follow along at a much slower gait.

Jess had the feeling that he should have anticipated this when he'd seen Slattery racing away from the Castle Rock area, and yet, because he was only now beginning to understand just how dangerous Mike Slattery was, he did not entirely blame himself.

As they went along, Hugh Shannon, who had been riding twisted in his saddle, straightened full around to call out: "Clem's comin' with the posse!"

Jess paid no attention to this. He angled for creek shade and thereafter followed the willows straight south to that broad, sandy road leading into Big B's yard. As he and Hugh came boiling onward toward the ranch buildings, they saw no one in sight at all. But as soon as the clattering rattle of their approach traveled ahead where others heard it, men came tumbling from the bunkhouse with guns up and ready.

Jess called out sharply, identifying himself. He left his horse on the fly and ran on to the house where his mother and Margaret Lawton came quickly out onto the verandah to meet him.

"John found me at the squatter camp," he said breathlessly, and turned a slow look toward the front of the house, where the raw wood showed whitely, splintered by bullets.

His mother said: "Come inside, son. They might return."

Margaret Lawton's cheeks were pale, and her eyes looked black and enormous. "I rode over to see if I could help care for the little girl, Jess. I hadn't been here ten minutes . . ."

"Thank the Lord they didn't catch you like they did Slim." Jess stepped over the threshold and halted. There were two smashed lamps and a perforated fruit bowl littering the floor. His lips went flat, and his gaze turned icelike.

"How bad off is Doc Hartman?" he asked, and his mother beckoned him along to a spare bedroom.

Here, Jacob Hartman was sitting on the edge of a bed, examining a bad gash in his upper left leg. He glanced up testily when Jess entered and said caustically: "Without a damned word of warning. They went over that yard out there like strong heart Injun warriors. I was on the porch. Before I could get to cover, they shot me."

Jess watched Hartman's hands work at a stained bandage, removing it in favor of fresh dressings. "Where was Billy Ray," he asked, "and Samuel?"

"At the bunkhouse with the men," his mother said. "Jess, it happened so fast, no one knew what was going on before those men were over the yard and gone. As Jacob said . . . 'It was like a slashing Indian raid.'" She looked down at the medical man. "Tell him about Slim," she directed.

Hartman grunted and went on with his bandaging.

"John and a couple of your other men found him and brought him to the house, Jess. Evidently, they came up behind him. He's out at the bunkhouse now."

"How bad off is he?"

"He'll live, but he won't be forking a horse for a long time. One bullet darned near tore his right ear off. It was that one that knocked him senseless. The second slug broke his left arm. The third one went through his left lower leg, through the horse he was riding, and then went through the leather of his right boot. When we were putting him to bed, it fell out of the boot." Hartman winced and continued his bandaging. He looked up swiftly, saying: "Well, are you going to stand there . . . or do something!"

Jess faced Margaret Lawton. The beautiful girl's face was only now beginning to regain its color.

"How is Linda Louise?" he asked.

Margaret took his hand, led him out to the hallway and down its cool gloominess.

Behind them Dr. Hartman said angrily: "Don't stand there, Mary! Fetch me a dram of whiskey."

They heard Jess's mother make a tart rejoinder to this demand.

When Jess entered Linda Louise's room, the little girl's big brown eyes viewed him soberly, then filled with warm relief. "I wanted for you to be here," she said, when Jess eased down upon the side of her bed and took up one hand to hold. "Jess, I was real scairt."

"Are you all right, though?" he asked, and Linda Louise nodded up at him.

"No one told me what happened, Jess. Are my pa and Billy Ray all right?"

"They're all right, I'm sure," said Jess, and arose. "You just rest. Margaret will stay with you, honey, and I'll be back as soon as I can."

"But what happened?" Linda Louise persisted.

"Some men raided the ranch," he replied, and passed back out into the hallway. He was moving down it when Margaret's voice halted him. He turned. She swept up to him, looking fearful, looking anxious.

"What will you do, Jess? Listen, send one of your men for my father and our riders."

Jess put out a hand to touch her hair, her cheek, and let that hand lightly rest upon her shoulder. "Don't worry," he said. "It won't happen again." He bent swiftly, kissed her mouth, and ran on, leaving the house to pace swiftly to the bunkhouse.

Here, when he entered, several excited cowboys began speaking at once. John Burr, who had gotten back only moments before, shot a black look around, and the room became silent.

Jess went to a lower bunk where lay a tousle-headed man who had just finished speaking to Hugh Shannon.

He said: "Howdy, Slim. Doc says you'll make it all right."

"Yeah," the wounded cowboy replied dryly, "with one ear off and a limp."

"Did you get a look at them before they shot you?"

"Not a real good look, Jess, but I recognized two of Circle S's riders. I don't know their names, but I've seen 'em in town. I didn't see Slattery though. In fact I didn't see much of anything before the sky fell on me."

Perkins reached up past the huge bandage around his head to rumple a tuft of protruding hair. "What in the doggoned hell," he exclaimed perplexedly, "brought all that on, anyway? I was ridin' home, mindin' my own darned business, when all at once here they come, ridin' like the devil, and then they opened up on me."

"John can explain," said Jess, turning toward his ranch foreman.

Burr was standing there, lost in frowning thought. He said plaintively: "What did Mike figure to accomplish . . . doin' a damned fool thing like that, Jess?"

Hugh Shannon was making a cigarette and watching Jess over his fingertips. He saw Jess suddenly snap erect as though invisible fingers had slapped his face. Hugh turned instantly still and watchful.

Jess went to the doorway and stood there, head cocked, listening. Then he relaxed as that familiar big swarm of possemen came down into the yard.

Hugh completed his smoke, lit up, and exhaled. He watched the possemen head for the water trough, all but old Clem Brite who stepped wearily up into shade and dropped down upon the bunkhouse steps, mopping at his beet-red face and looking slowly around at the many bullet scars upon those Big B buildings.

A shuffling tall figure came forth from around the side of the bunkhouse. It was Samuel Patton. He was being trailed by a blue-eyed shadow who, upon seeing Jess standing there, cut around his father to dart onward and halt next to Jess, looking relieved and suddenly content.

Jess felt Billy Ray's fingers steal into his palm. He held that damp small hand, gazing at Samuel.

"I was down at the creek bathing," said Samuel to those solemn faces. "By the time I got dressed, it was all over." Samuel started away. "I've got to go to the house now," he added.

"She's all right!" called Jess. "I just came from there. She wasn't hurt."

Samuel slowed, he turned and put his thankful look back at Jess, then he nodded and walked on.

Clem Brite said: "Hugh, don't hog your tobacco. Give me some."

Hugh complied, and old Clem went to work with both hands.

The Big B riders all filed out onto the bunkhouse's little porch and stood there in glum silence.

When Clem had his smoke going, he leaned back to look upward. "Jess, he's plumb gone crazy," he said. "It's got to be that. He can't get away with a thing like this. Folks'll be up in arms after him when they hear about this raid, too. Bad enough to shoot Blaine Richards. But this . . . with women in the house . . ." Brite did not finish, he dropped his head forward and wagged it bitterly.

There were now over thirty men standing in the yard at Big B's bunkhouse. They were in the main quiet and thoughtful. A number of the Hereford possemen lingered at that watering trough to care for their own and their horses' thirsts.

Jess, having surveyed the results of Slattery's slashing attack at Big B, was plumbing his mind for the reasons of this. Very gradually, as the sun began to drop off westerly, a suspicion formed strongly in his head.

Finally, he said to Clem Brite: "Send your possemen to the other ranches, Clem. Have them gather riders and head for that squatter camp at Castle Rock."

Brite killed his cigarette and arose stiffly off the bunkhouse steps. "All right," he said, then started violently. "Jess! You figure he went back up there?"

"Yes. He struck here to draw us all down here. What else could it be? He didn't stay around, just made that one murderous charge, then ran on. That's got to be it, Clem."

Around them men began speaking. Some turned to their mounts, prepared to step astride.

Hugh Shannon's quiet, corn-husk dry voice said over this little turmoil: "No big rush, boys. No big rush at all." He gazed at Jess and smiled. "Slattery's gun crew is due for one helluva surprise when they brace those mountaineers. They already know those men can shoot a long ways and dead straight. Now they're goin' to find out just how many of them there are, back in those little aspen trees."

Clem rolled his brows together over this, though not nearly as calm over the prospects as Jess and Hugh Shannon were. He called off a number of names, then said to these men: "Ride for the other ranches. Tell everyone you see what's happening and what has already happened. Then say the rest of us'll be up at Castle Rock waiting for them."

Clem made a curt gesture with one outflung hand. "Go on, and don't waste a lot of time at any one place."

These messengers left the yard all in a rushing body of riders. They split off from each other beyond Big B's main gate.

In the yard Jess turned to John Burr. "Hugh and I will need fresh horses. I think you'd better stay here with our men, John, just in case Slattery's got something else up his sleeve."

Burr moved off toward the corral. He called to a cowboy lounging in the shade to accompany him.

The other men went to their own animals, mounted up, and sat there in hot afternoon sunlight waiting for Jess and Hugh to join them.

As old Brite got back into his saddle, he let off a loud groan, then fell to steadily cursing all this hard-riding discomfort.

CHAPTER TWELVE

They rode back toward Castle Rock with less haste than before. Afternoon was shimmering around them, its heat dry and pulsing. Distances were hazed as though by smoke, and a redness permeated the atmosphere from that sinking great orb off in the shadowy west.

Clem Brite took out a large gold watch and studied its hands, then gravely returned it to his pocket. "Four hours till dark," he said, "and I don't like the idea of more men comin' up to join the fight when it's too dark to make out friend from foe." He looked around at Jess. "A man who gets killed by mistake is just as dead as one killed on purpose."

Jess, though, had other thoughts about more riders coming up. "If we outnumber them at least five to one, I think they'll quit."

Around them the possemen plodded along, desultorily speaking and smoking, their voices sounding tired from all this.

Hugh Shannon spurred on ahead a ways, then returned to say: "By golly, I didn't hear any gunfire."

He and Jess exchanged a look. Clem Brite screwed his face up in puzzlement.

"Jess, maybe we figured wrong. Maybe he ain't going up there at all. Maybe he was waiting for us to leave your place so's he could renew that attack."

This might have caused consternation for Jess with its logic, but at that moment they all heard a ripple of far-off gunfire.

"We got that answered now," muttered old Brite, and put a squinted look sunward. "We better go a mite faster," he muttered. "That sun's going to be gone before long."

They eased over into a loose gallop and held to this gait until the cliff face, saffron now and shadowed, clearly showed. Then they heard that gunfire begin to swell.

Hugh said: "They haven't been up here very long, Jess. Sounds like they've just opened up."

"It's the other guns I'm trying to hear," stated Jess.

They all rode along swiftly separating the sharper, more stinging crack of those long rifles from the flatter and duller smash of saddle guns. Then, onward another half mile, they sighted Slattery's riders far out, some kneeling, some standing beside their mounts, and all using that identical strategy they'd used earlier of shooting high and dropping bullets into the aspen grove.

"Won't hurt anybody like that," observed old Brite. "You could fire at a man like that all day, and he likely would never find it out."

But something had struck Jess. "That's only about half Slattery's crew," he observed. After a brief pause, he then said: "Hell, those men aren't trying to hit anyone. They're just trying to hold the mountaineers' attention. Slattery's up to something else."

"Well," barked old Clem Brite, closing his face down harshly around his thoughts, "one thing we can damned well do, and that's interrupt whatever he's got in mind and keep him busy for a while along with it." He waved an arm. "Come on."

They broke out of their easy pacing and went careening onward toward that thin line of Circle S men, who were so occupied with their firing toward the aspen grove they failed to heed the sound of many horses coming up swiftly until someone among them shouted. This was a startled, ripped-out sound.

It brought the Circle S men around in a new direction all at once. Instantly, gunfire flashed southward.

Old Clem Brite swore a mighty curse and yelled viciously: "Give it to them!" The next second his horse jackknifed under him, and Brite went pinwheeling through the air to land hard twenty feet onward.

At once the men around him yanked back hard, not so much to avoid running over old Clem as to run away before that slamming gunfire.

Jess got to Clem and helped him to sit up. Hugh Shannon grabbed Jess's horse and ran on to put his own and Jess's animal between those mounting-up Circle S men and his two friends upon the ground.

"You hurt?" cried Jess, over the sudden eruption of answering gunfire from the possemen.

Old Clem put a wilting glare upon Jess. "Hell no," he snorted. "I do this all the time. For fun. Now help me up."

Hugh Shannon fell back as Jess and Clem retreated on foot. Jess gave Brite into the care of others and retrieved his horse. He was fighting mad.

The Circle S men were now beginning to break away eastward. They swung now and then to let off a shot, more in the hope of discouraging pursuit, Jess thought, than because they expected to hit anyone. He looked around, saw Hugh and ten or twelve others also watching those fleeing men, and called out: "Come on, they want to fight! Let's oblige them!"

Jess's horse sprang far ahead and lit running. Its rider turned to see how many of the possemen would follow. Over half of them came after him, and all of these men had their weapons out now, up and ready.

From the aspen grove came a distant volley of long-rifle fire. Jess watched the fleeing Circle S men, saw none fall or falter, and figured the distance was too great. He heard men crying out, too, but spent no time seeking these people until Hugh Shannon ran up to him, gesturing frantically with a naked Winchester and yelling over the other sounds in the afternoon.

"Jess, it's the squatters. Look!"

Jess swung his head.

Tolivar's men were standing well out in plain sight from the aspen grove. They were gesticulating furiously eastward. Jess did not at once understand, but then, when the Circle S men onward began to slow, to let loose an infrequent shot, it struck Jess instantly what the mountaineers were trying to convey to him.

He set his horse up in a long slide and yelled to the riders piling up behind him: "Ambush! Hold up! They're trying to lead us where the rest of Slattery's gunmen are."

Hugh Shannon stopped four hard-riding possemen who kept on going. He accomplished this by simply firing his pistol rapidly into the air behind them. When they ducked low and looked back, Hugh waved a peremptory arm at them.

Onward, the Circle S men now stopped entirely. They sat their yonder saddles looking back at Jess and his party. One of them tried a long shot. It fell short a hundred feet and made dust spurt.

On eastward, where the valley began to close in toward that cliff face and the twisting old road that traversed it, there was a great jumble of large rocks. Here, as he strained for movement,

Jess saw Slattery's men move naked carbines. The sun struck down upon these weapons, sending out quick, short flashes of reddening light.

"Clever," growled Hugh Shannon. "Real clever. If we'd followed those riders, they'd have led us right down the line of rocks for their friends to knock us out of the saddle like tin soldiers."

But Jess, letting all the possemen come up and mill around him and Hugh, was considering those onward rocks. Behind them rose up nearly vertical hillsides. These terminated three hundred feet up where a thin fringe of pines stood.

"Not so damned clever," he said to Hugh. "Listen, you go get those squatters and take them around to the north from their camp. Have them hold the northward route."

Hugh nodded, not quite understanding but willing.

Jess selected a townsman from that group of men on his left. "You take half of your Hereford crew on south, and close off the retreat route that way."

Now Hugh understood. He said, in a swift way: "Hell yes! Slattery's put himself with his back to a wall."

Hugh started to rein away as Clem Brite came up on foot, using his carbine as a cane. He said something sharp to the crowding horsemen, who drew their animals back for him to stamp past on his way to halt at Jess's stirrup and glare ahead where those Circle S men still sat their saddles, watching.

"Clem," said Jess. "Take half your town posse and string it out across the plain right here. I've already made arrangements to bottle Slattery up on his right and his left. That way we'll have him pinned down."

Brite considered this plan. He eventually nodded grim approval, turned, and barked names of men who drew clear of their companions and rallied around him.

Jess nodded at Hugh. Shannon at once spun away to go loping

toward the aspen grove. The first half of the posse went south behind their leader, stiffly trotting.

Jess remained there with Clem and the balance of the men from Hereford. "It might work," he said, sounding not altogether confident. "If we can hold them in those doggoned rocks until the other cowmen get up here . . . it will work."

"Of course it will," snapped Clem, gingerly rubbing a leg. "Why wouldn't it?"

Instead of answering that, Jess slowly turned and gazed at the dropping sun. His meaning was amply clear to all who saw him do this. In the darkness, after daylight ended, Slattery's gun crew stood a good chance of escaping.

Brite, understanding this now, mumbled dourly to those near him. "Keep sharp watch, confound it! We'll likely have the other ranchers up here before sunset anyway."

Jess stood hipshot beside his horse, looking toward the aspen grove. Hugh had disappeared there, and now there was not a sound anywhere. He strained to catch movement but saw none. A solitary thin and spiraling lift of smoke rose up above the grove where people had been preparing their evening meal. This trickle was entirely too diluted though to be coming from a tended fire. Jess was sure the mountaineers were all concentrating on other things now and for the moment forgetting their stomachs.

He swung to look southward. That other half of Brite's posse was hard down the land. The riders looked small and barely moving. As he watched, they changed course and began angling inward toward the mountain flank.

A yell from those watching Circle S men on ahead caught his attention. These men were no longer sitting there watching. They had at last divined what their enemies were up to. And now they were trotting steadily back toward the rocks where the balance of their outfit was.

"Dunces," mumbled Clem, his shaggy old brows shifted down thunderously. "Sure took 'em long enough to figure this out." He looked over at Jess. "Say, what the hell was Mike up to, anyway, having half his crew dropping bullets into the grove like that?"

"The same thing they tried on us," came back Jess's short answer. "They were baiting the squatters out of the trees by appearing few in numbers. Then they'd have run ahead of them as they tried to do with us . . . and led 'em right down that first row of rocks to be picked off one at a time."

"Haw!" grunted Clem. "It plumb backfired." He swung to search the descending soft light for signs of newcomers. His tone changed abruptly, becoming testy again. "What in hell's keeping the other cowmen, anyway?"

Jess was thinking other thoughts. He estimated Slattery's men in the yonder rocks to number not more than twenty and more plausibly, fifteen. He and Clem had with them out in the center of the plain, six possemen. He thought that Slattery could determine how many men were north of his stronghold quite easily, by drawing their single-shot musket fire, and counting the fired weapons.

If Slattery did this, he would know at once that Hugh Shannon and his mountaineers were too numerous for Slattery to fight past. Slattery could also determine the number of possemen south of him in the same manner, and again, he would inevitably decide that riding straight ahead where Clem Brite, Jess, and six others stood guard, would be his best route of escape.

Jess did not communicate these thoughts to the men around him. He instead suggested that one posseman take their horses well back beyond gun range and remain with the animals. After seeing to this, he detailed the men to positions well within sight of one another but a good hundred yards apart. His final instructions were for the possemen to make no noise and to concentrate on listening for any attempt of Slattery's gunmen to leave the rocks.

Clem Brite, the last to walk away, said to Jess with a sharp look: "Glad you finally took over. I knew you would sooner or later, but I'd have just as soon not had to take that fall to get you to do it."

Jess watched Brite hobble off, still using his carbine as a walking aid. Then Jess squatted upon the ground and waited. Behind him the sun dropped steadily toward the highest westerly peak, and when it ultimately struck there, it seemed to explode, pouring a red-golden light in a rushing flash down over the plain, the mountains, and the north-south sweep of Absaroka Valley.

Summertime dusk, though, was a lingering long time of quietude, of cooling earth and faint soft light. Ordinarily, it was to Jess the most beautiful time of day. Now though, he considered its remaining daylight as something standing between himself and very real danger.

He turned, while he could see well enough, and ran a probing look southward, hoping to sight a dust banner made by oncoming horsemen. He saw nothing at all but lengthening shadows taking their giant strides onward over his valley from the mountain heights, bringing closer and closer the darkness he was now certain Mike Slattery and his silent gunmen were also awaiting.

Northward came a long and musical call. Jess fixed his attention upon the aspen grove, but nothing occurred, and he concluded that this cry had no immediate meaning. He sat on, holding his carbine and waiting for—he knew not what.

CHAPTER THIRTEEN

Darkness came reluctantly, and still that silence ran on. Clem hobbled up where Jess squatted to say: "I don't understand what's taking the ranchers so long."

"They'll be taking it careful," answered Jess, and returned his attention forward. "You better go back, Clem. If Slattery figures to break out, he'll be doing it pretty quick now."

Brite started away. "A full moon would help," he muttered to himself, then faded out into the darkness.

A short while after this, a solitary rifle shot sounded ahead of Jess and off to his left. He waited for a repetition of this sound in order to place the rifleman's location, but there was only that one quick shot. He thought, though, that the squatters were edging southward toward Slattery's stronghold. He could imagine Hugh Shannon urging them to do this.

The stillness ran on again. Jess tried to estimate how much time had elapsed since they'd returned to Castle Rock. It seemed, in some ways, to be no more than an hour. In other ways it could have been a lifetime. He was getting to his feet when, several hundred yards south of him, a sudden flurry of gunfire broke out. He knew at once what this presaged: Slattery was making his move. He was seeking to get out of the surround. As Jess turned fully in the direction of those shots, he knew instinctively that Slattery had, during daylight, seen that only six possemen, Clem Brite, and himself, cut off his westward escape, and that he had elected to fight past this thin enemy line.

The gunfire increased now. Jess, running toward it, sighted red-orange muzzle blast. When he heard horsemen charging down the night, he dropped to one knee, awaiting a target.

But Slattery's crew was veering farther southward, their gun flashes proving that this was so. Jess sprang up and ran on another hundred yards. Here, he found a badly shaken posseman shooting into the darkness from a prone position.

The man swung a frightened face as Jess came down beside him. He gasped: "They come slippin' up. I didn't even hear 'em. Then all of a sudden . . . there they were."

"Come on," Jess snapped, and jumped up to continue running southward. Behind him other possemen were converging upon the gunfight.

Farther south the fight was swirling southeastward. Here Jess found that someone had brought up the possemen's horses, and four of them were mounted and carrying the battle to Slattery. Someone close by shouted his name. Jess turned. An anxious man pushed a set of reins into his hand, then turned away to mount his own horse. As Jess watched, this man spun his horse, then started forward, and almost at once a bullet came out of darkness to pluck him from the saddle.

Slattery, encountering stiffer resistance than he'd obviously thought he would run into, and facing mounted men who repeatedly ran at his crew, fired and fled. The he turned abruptly northward, running the full length of Jess's line as though to break out around the possemen northwestward.

It was difficult for a while to determine in the night which set of horse sounds belonged to Slattery and which set belonged to the possemen. Jess accomplished this by concentrating on the closed-up mass of riders. His own men were too scattered to be moving in such an orderly fashion. He heard those speeding animals approaching, hauled back, and unloaded from his horse, knelt, and snugged back his carbine.

But before he got up where Jess was, Slattery took his big chance. He wheeled abruptly to his left and went crashing westward at full speed, running through and beyond the posse's thin line.

Jess heard someone come up close by and, panting, drop down to fire. It was Clem Brite. He recognized the older man's gravel tones as Clem fired and cursed and fired again, aiming, as Jess also did, by sound only.

Then that shuddering racket of running horses diminished beyond carbine range, and Jess straightened up, grounded his gun, and called out: "Rally here, boys! Rally on the sound of my voice!"

Clem was the first one up. He glared into the obscure west, and his leathery lips moved but no sounds came. Another posseman also ambled up. He was reloading as he walked. A third and fourth man arrived, both mounted and leading someone's saddle horse. The man who had reloaded his carbine went close to squint at this animal, then, taking the reins, letting out an "ahhh," before saying to the mounted men around him: "He ran off at the first shot."

After a time a fifth posseman came up. He was limping and he told the others that the sixth man was down, badly hurt, a good distance to the south.

"Shot?" someone asked.

The limping man wagged his head. "Run over. He was lyin' on the ground to my right. If he'd stayed down, he'd have been all right. But when Slattery's boys come on, he fired and jumped up. One of the Circle S men ran right into him. It broke his leg, I think, but it also made the horse fall." The posseman paused to ease weight off his leg. "Twisted my damned ankle in a chuckhole," he said. "Anyway, when that horse went down, I run over to the rider and took him a cut over the skull." The man made a careless southward jerk of his head. "He's lyin' back down there, too. I don't know whether I brained him or not, but he sure never moved after I hit him."

Jess said curtly: "Come on." And he headed southward.

The others went along with him. They found the injured man sitting up and using strips of his shirt to bind his broken leg. Everyone but Clem Brite and Jess remained to help this man. Jess and Clem went on where that other lumpy shape lay sprawled.

The gunman groaned when Jess knelt to roll him over upon his back, but he otherwise made no intelligible sound or movement. Jess worked over this gunman, trying to bring him round. He was unsuccessful though and eventually gave up when Clem tugged at his sleeve.

"Someone's coming," whispered Brite, indicating a sound coming from the east, and holding his shaggy head to one side. The pair of them immediately went back where the other possemen had also heard those sounds of men in the darkness, and at a hand signal from Jess, everyone got down upon the ground.

Those approaching men suddenly halted. Jess could hear them speaking very quietly together, uncertain about something ahead of them. He heard one recognizable voice speak over the others and relaxed to call forward: "Hugh, come on up. It's Jess."

Shannon answered this summons with a relieved curse, and

shortly thereafter he came striding into sight, trailed by old Moses Tolivar and the swinging along silhouettes of Tolivar's men.

"Did they get past you?" Hugh asked at once. Jess said: "Yes. There's one of them lying over there. I think he's got a cracked skull. One of our men's got a broken leg, too."

Old Tolivar went over to the injured posseman and examined his leg gravely. He then turned and said: "Gabe, fix this feller up, will you." Then he got back to his feet to step clear as a lanky, graying man moved past, got down upon his knees, put aside his long rifle, and began at once untying the shirt strips the injured man had wrapped around his leg.

"What you doin'?" complained the hurt man.

"Your leg's got to be splinted," drawled the mountaineer, then added to some of his friends who were watching: "See can you find that there gunman's musket, boys. We'll use the stock fer splints." He shifted to draw forth a wickedly long knife and neatly slit the injured man's trousers. In the same casual tone he said: "Now, mister, you jest rest easy. I've patched up more busted bones than you can shake a stick at."

Moses Tolivar leaned upon his rifle in front of Jess. He said dryly: "They's a dead one yonder in them rocks. Believe he was fixin' to run away from his friends. Anyway, he come slippin' along north-ward . . . and one o' my boys riz up an' shot him plumb square."

That, thought Jess, accounted for that solitary rifle shot he'd heard some time before. Then Tolivar was speaking again, and at the same time running crooked fingers through his great shaggy beard in a comblike fashion.

"There's some riders comin' up the valley," he said. "We heard 'em when we were back yonder at the mountain right after Mistah Slattery pulled out. They was a considerable ways south, though."

Seeing Jess's inquiring look, old Tolivar explained: "Sound carries easy in the night, an' it bounces off cliffs like that one which was behind us. We heard 'em back there easy 'nough, but out here, a feller can't hear 'em at all."

Clem Brite chirped delightedly when a posseman came walking out of the westward darkness, leading a horse. The man silently handed the reins of this beast to Brite, and passed on with a minimal explanation: "Went scoutin' out a ways and found this critter wanderin' around lost. Probably belongs to that gunman with the busted head."

Jess could now hear ridden horses approaching slowly, cautiously, and turned in the direction of this sound. At his side Moses Tolivar gravely drew forth a twist of cured tobacco, worried off a nubbin of it, pouched this into his cheek, and began to methodically chew. The gaunt mountaineer had completed splinting that broken leg and now helped hoist the injured townsman to his one good leg. Two other possemen lent this man their arms for support. He hobbled up to Jess and Tolivar with a sweaty, ashen face, and stood there with everyone else, waiting for those oncoming riders to appear.

It was a long wait. The approaching cowmen sent ahead two scouts before coming in close. And even after it had been determined who that body of men were they could easily detect by cigarette tips and silhouetted movement, the ranchers still delayed their arrival until after they had split up and come ahead in a surrounding fashion.

This annoyed Clem. He called tartly and profanely who the men with him were, and after that the ranchers converged and dismounted.

The townsmen who had been sent out to bring up this cowman force went at once to their friends, and a great many voices erupted simultaneously. Jess and Clem Brite were approached by two older men from south of the town of Hereford; these were Jack Parsons of the Turkey Track outfit and Les Coulter of the Pinetree Ranch.

Jess explained what had thus far occurred and introduced the cattlemen to Moses Tolivar.

The possemen were stiff and prudent around Tolivar's squatters. They heeded everything Jess and Clem Brite told them, but it was evident that they had their private opinions, for they did not speak to the mountaineers unless spoken to, and ultimately, when old Tolivar suggested that everyone return with him and his men to the camp at Castle Rock Spring, the cowmen did not at once agree.

But they ignored their opinion when old Clem and Jess led the way. Then they trailed along, leading their horses and staying slightly apart.

Noticing this, Hugh Shannon sidled up to Jess to say: "Mike did his work real well, the way Jack and Les and their riders are actin'."

But Jess seemed untroubled. After a couple of minutes, he reminded Hugh that all of the ranchers, including Hugh and himself, had initially felt pretty much the same way. "They'll come around, Hugh, if Tolivar agrees not to squat in our valley."

Hugh made a lopsided little smile. "I doubt if we could get him to stay if we begged him to . . . after all this."

* * * * *

At the squatter camp, a surprising number of women came from the wagons to light lamps and pass silently among the men to see whether or not all had returned. There was a little talk here, and Jess saw Hugh Shannon spring forward to again assist the tall girl with auburn hair and jet-black eyes as she poked up the cooking fire and readied several coffeepots.

The wounded posseman was made comfortable upon a straw pallet, and after a while several of Tolivar's young men came into camp with the injured gunman among them. This man had still not regained consciousness.

The mountaineer who had so deftly set that broken leg made a thoughtful examination of this gunman and said he would have to be cared for by a medical doctor. That he appeared to have a cracked skull.

In the increasing cheeriness of that stoked-up fire, the men talked, drank coffee, and examined their arms.

Jess, speaking aside to Les Coulter, Moses Tolivar, Jack Parsons, and Clem Brite, said he thought they should hunt Slattery down now, instead of awaiting daylight.

Tolivar said nothing to this, but awaited the decision of the valley cowmen. When they ultimately agreed, Tolivar then also did. He departed to direct his young men to get their horses.

When Tolivar was no longer within earshot, Les Coulter, looking carefully around the mountaineer camp, said: "They sure are a strange lot . . . but, by golly, did you ever see such politeness?"

Parsons said to Clem somewhat hesitantly: "After Slattery . . . we'll have to take them on."

Brite snorted. "Not I," he affirmed stoutly. "I'm not going to fight these people."

"But, hell, Clem," protested the rancher. "They're squatters. They're out to steal someone's land."

Jess said: "Why not wait until they actually do that, before talking fight?"

Parsons looked from Clem to Jess. He said: "Isn't that what they're doin' right now? This here spring belongs to Circle S, doesn't it?"

"They came down out of the northward mountains, Jack," explained Jess. "They had to camp somewhere. They didn't know all Absaroka Valley was deeded land. They figured it might have homesteading possibilities."

"They better be told different then," replied Parsons.

"They've been told."

"Then what are they still doin' here?"

Clem Brite swore. Then he said irritably: "They never had a chance to pull out. Slattery come a-helling and ever since then they been fighting just like the rest of us have been doing." He stomped away from that little group to stand moodily by the fire.

CHAPTER FOURTEEN

Moses Tolivar returned to the place in those shifting shadows near the fire where Jess and the other cattlemen stood. He looked quietly into their faces, guessed what had been discussed in his absence, and said: "If that there offer still holds 'bout guidin' us on south where that big plain is, we'll be plumb obliged to you all."

Clem Brite limped back to this little group. He put a reproving look upon Les Coulter and Jack Parsons, but held his silence.

"When this other thing is over," exclaimed Jess, "we'll show you that prairie, Mr. Tolivar."

Hugh Shannon ambled up, looked at those silent faces, and said quietly to Jess: "Everyone's tanked up on coffee, the horses are rested. Maybe we'd better ride."

As the cowmen were turning toward their mounts, a man came hobbling in through the trees. He put a gloomy face upon everyone, saying: "Fine lot you fellers are. I could've bled to death out there."

Until Jess got a good look at this man, he had forgotten entirely having seen him get shot out of his saddle after handing Jess the reins to his animal. Now he went forward as though to help the limping man, but the posseman growled: "Leave me be. Fine lot you fellers are." He went dourly past Jess and the others and on to the fire where he lowered himself gingerly to a log there, pushed out both legs, and began rubbing them.

"Got shot plumb out of my saddle an' there I lay with scrambled brains, and you fellers just rode on off and let me lie there."

Hugh Shannon's darkly somber face gradually creased into a smile. He knew this townsman and went over now to gaze down at him. "Harry," he said, "you don't look shot to me. You look a little stiff is all."

"A little stiff!" exploded the posseman. "Why doggone you, Hugh Shannon . . . a bullet hit me square on the belt buckle and flung me off my horse like a sledgehammer. I lit spread out and liked to split myself in two." The man sprang up, winced from this, and used both hands to show his buckle. Indeed, the metal was badly dented inward from a hard impact.

Hugh looked, nodded, and continued to look amused.

"That proves somethin'," he mused. "That a belt's good for somethin' besides holdin' up a man's britches, maybe. Or that . . ."

"You," snarled the indignant posseman, cutting fiercely across Shannon's words, "can go plumb to hell!"

Some of the men laughed, and others had sly comments to make. Even old Clem and Moses Tolivar exchanged a twinkling wink. All this served to vanquish that thin but persisting line of stiffness between Tolivar's squatters and the Absaroka Valley cowmen.

Jess called out: "Let's ride!"

To which the irate posseman over at the fire exclaimed firmly that he'd be damned if he'd ride with such callous men again and went down very gingerly again upon the log.

Tolivar's men came into firelight leading horses. Jess looked at these wagon animals, said nothing, but he and Shannon exchanged a look. Some of the cowmen and their riders solemnly considered the mountaineers' harness horses from impassive faces.

Jess lifted his reins, waited until old Tolivar was safely upon his animal, then eased out forward. Around him nearly sixty riders passed on out of the aspen grove to the valley floor, and here, at long last, there was watery moonlight to see by.

Clem Brite shook a fist at that serene overhead disc and plodded along, looking disgruntled and yeasty.

Jess, heading southeasterly toward Slattery's home ranch, made his first mistake here, and yet it was conceivably an understandable mistake, for beside him rode Coulter and Parsons and Hugh Shannon, and each of them accepted this route of travel without protest or comment.

In fact, after they had progressed downcountry nearly two miles, Shannon said: "We better split up. Part of us approach like we're ridin' now and the other part come in from the west . . . just in case."

Clem said tartly: "We had enough pussyfooting for one night, consarn it. Let's just bust in there and take our chances."

Jess responded mildly: "With a moon behind us, Clem, and only the Lord knows how many expert marksmen ahead of us?"

Clem subsided, riding grumpily along, trying without success to ease the discomfort to his injured ankle all this riding entailed.

When they were no more than a half mile from the Circle S, Moses Tolivar said: "I got some boys here who can out-Injun any redskin at slippin' along in the dark. If you're of a mind, I can send 'em on ahead."

Jess agreed to this at once.

Old Tolivar turned his clumsy horse aside, spoke to several of his mountaineers, and these men at once pushed on ahead of the main party in an ungainly, shambling trot.

Jess and Hugh exchanged another look, said nothing, and continued riding along, all the time watching those lanky men upon their big awkward horses, fade out in the yonder gloom.

Tolivar eased up to ride stirrup with Clem Brite. These two, in spite of their differences, not only in background and size, but in their tempers as well, seemed entirely compatible. They spoke back and forth in low tones—Clem's tone quick, sharp, pointed, and Moses Tolivar's voice soft, drawling, and unperturbed.

Otherwise, the men of this large posse, having until this day not known one another, were taciturn in each other's presence, watchful and polite in a formal way. One or two of the cattlemen aside from Clem Brite, such as Hugh Shannon and Jess Bennett, were at ease among the mountaineers. Hugh was particularly affable, having found a young squatter who could, and would, tell him what he wished to know about that handsome, tall girl with the jet eyes and thickly wavy auburn hair.

In this manner the posse came closer to Slattery's Circle S, allies out of necessity but as yet nothing more than that. Willing to support one another in battle, but unwilling to let down their personal and individual guards any more than that.

Suddenly, out of the onward night, a man appeared as though out of the ground. He rose up almost under the hoofs of the foremost horses and stood there, tall and calm and holding his rifle crossways in front of his body in the crook of one arm.

"No one at that ranch yonder," this mountaineer reported to Jess, when the cavalcade halted. "Unless they're hidin' there . . . waitin'."

Moses Tolivar came up and leaned forward to see and identify this scout. He said: "Where's Josh?"

The scout twisted from the waist and looked southward. "Still a-lookin'," he said succinctly. "I come back to hold you fellers up a spell . . . until Josh comes along." This man looked calmly at Tolivar.

"But I had a pretty close look, Moses. There are no critters in the corrals, and the buildings are dark. I don't allow that Slattery feller led his crew here at all."

Tolivar settled back. "We'll wait," he pronounced, and put a steady look upon Jess as though considering it possible Jess might disagree with this.

But Jess did not. He was beginning to have that uneasy feeling again. A number of thoughts ran through his mind. He turned, beckoned Hugh Shannon up, and said to him: "I've got a bad feeling about this. Ride down toward Big B and keep your eyes and ears wide open."

Hugh stiffened. "You figure he went back over there?" he asked, in a sharp tone. "Good Lord!"

"He went somewhere, Hugh. If he's not at Circle S, where else would he be?"

Tolivar had an idea about this. "Back at the aspen grove," he said. "He'll be waitin' to hit some place, and maybe it's our camp . . . with the women and children there 'most alone."

Jess saw other pale faces grow still, grow speculative, after Tolivar finished speaking.

He said to Hugh Shannon: "Go on. If you detect anything, come back here."

And after Hugh went off in a swift lope, Jess faced Tolivar and spoke again in the same crisp voice. "Take your men and go back to the camp. Stay there . . . even if Slattery isn't there, you stay there and protect your people. We have enough cowmen here to do what's got to be done."

Tolivar nodded. He was beginning to drag his horse around when a second man came up to them from the out of the night.

"It's Josh!" cried this newcomer, identifying himself. Then he stopped and sat his horse, gazing ahead at old Tolivar with a perplexed look upon his face.

"There's a crippled-up old man at that Circle S place. He was sleepin' in their bunkhouse. I figure he'd likely be the cook. Outside of him though, there's not a soul there." The man shifted position in his saddle, before continuing to speak. "Mose, I don't much admire the way these folks fight. I cal'clate we'd best hightail it back to our womenfolk."

"We're going," said Tolivar, and completed pulling his horse around. He nodded at Jess and Clem Brite, said nothing until just before he rode away, then he directed his words to old Clem: "If you find Mistah Slattery an' you need us, send a rider to our camp. We'll come right along."

The mountaineers drew out of Jess's posse and went loping heavily back the way they had come.

Jess was beginning to form a plan. Before the diminishing sounds of those withdrawing riders was gone, he said to Clem Brite: "Take half the men and go on over to Circle S."

"But why the hell . . .?" protested Brite, before Jess could finish. "You just heard what that squatter fellow said."

"Listen a minute, will you, Clem?" demanded Jess, his tone turning sharp. "Take some men and go over. Get into position over there . . . and stay out of sight. Sooner or later Slattery will return to his home place . . . if he can. We don't want to have to dig him out of there . . . some of us'll get killed doing that. You be there to welcome him, if he comes."

Clem calmed slightly, seeing the logical merit of this. Others did also, and they murmured their approval. Clem bobbed his head up and down and commenced snapping out men's names. As he selected the riders to accompany him to Circle S these horsemen drew off from the main body of men and formed into a separate posse.

It wasn't long before old Brite rode off with his men without saying a word or throwing backward the customary offhand wave of an arm.

Someone said: "Old Clem's kind o' prickly tonight."

"He had a pretty hard fall for an old gaffer," stated another voice defensively.

The men said no more but returned their attention to Jess, who sat his saddle between Jack Parsons and Les Coulter.

The inactivity, the uncertainty, dragged at him. He felt tired, and his mending ribs did not long let him forget them. But he accepted a tobacco sack someone offered, twisted up a smoke, and lit it.

Somewhere in the night, Mike Slattery's twisted, crafty mind was working hard. If Jess went toward Big B, Slattery would turn up at the aspen grove. If he rode there, Slattery would run for Circle S. In the end, despite the anxiety in him, Jess sat on, smoking and waiting.

Slowly, he began to formulate a plan, though, and by the time Hugh Shannon came loping back to call out in a breathless way that Slattery was, indeed, attacking Big B, Jess had his strategy worked out.

He took Hugh's full report in silence, then he turned to Coulter saying briskly: "Ride for Circle S. Tell Clem where Slattery is and that I want him with me. Tell him to come at once to Big B . . . but not with his men."

"Huh?" said Coulter, looking bewildered.

"You stay with those men, Les. Have them spread out across the range between Big B and Circle S. We'll ride on to my place and join the fight there. Between this posse and my ranch crew, Slattery can't win, and he'll know it. I think he'll break off and make a run for it. If he does that, I want you and the men at Circle S to be out there across the trail he'll use. He won't be expecting you, Les. You ought to be able to stop him cold."

"Suppose," piped up a cowman deep in the midst of those dark and mounted cattlemen, "Slattery makes another run at the squatters . . . what then?"

Jess replied: "Tolivar can take care of him, if he tries that. He won't outnumber Mike by much, but he sure as the devil will have him out-gunned." Jess thought a moment, then faced Hugh Shannon to say: "Go on up there and tell Tolivar what's going on. Tell him that if he can spare any men to send them down to Les, where his riders'll be strung out across the plain. We don't want Slattery to ride through *us* again."

Shannon nodded and reined around. He eased out of the pressed-closely body of listening horsemen, then booted his animal over into a slow lope, heading north through the faint moonlight.

Over the sound of Shannon's fading hoof falls, Jess said quietly to Les Coulter: "Go on. Tell Clem to meet me at Big B. And remember . . . keep your men in position to pick up any Circle S gunman trying to slip off in the dark."

Coulter then rode away.

Jess then cast a final look at the silent, grim faces around him, threw up one arm, and brought it sharply down in a chopping fashion. This was the signal to head out. The cattlemen and the remaining members of the Hereford posse hooked their animals, and the entire party went southward and a little westward in a hard run.

Overhead, the moon and stars were brightening earth with a steady soft light. Night shapes and night shadows loomed up, then fell away, as these mounted men went swiftly past.

Shortly before they hit the Big B's road, that once-heard, never-forgotten sharp popping sound of gunfire came to each of them over the racket of their own progress. Every man among them who possessed a saddle gun now yanked it clear.

CHAPTER FIFTEEN

Slattery had the Big B cowboys pinned down in two places—the bunkhouse and the main ranch house. His gunmen were secreted everywhere else throughout Big B's yard. Several were in the log barn north of the bunkhouse. Others were in the smithy shed, the smokehouse, and behind such bulwarks as the parked roundup wagon, the harness shop, and the chicken house.

They had, Jess saw as he and his men cut sharply clear of the yard heading northward, been besieging Big B for some time. Even in the poor light, he could see smashed porch furniture, shattered windows, and pale gouges where bullets had struck.

At his arrival from the north, beyond the yard, a loud shout went up from some of the gunmen down in the yard, and a few hasty shots came toward Jess and his men.

Clem Brite, in the act of dismounting, winced from a near miss, hit the ground, and let off a stentorian roar of anger. After that close call, Clem limped up to Jess and said: "Get these damned horses out of range."

Jess was doing this as Clem came up. He had several possemen drive their animals far back. Then he called to the men: "Get down flat! Belly-down and take your time. And dammit, make your shots count!" To Clem he said: "You made good time."

Clem remained standing, squinting ahead in hard concentration.

It was impossible to see Slattery's men at all, but their gun flashes winked here and there, giving Jess's posse something to fire at.

"Get down, Clem!" cried Jess, as he strode toward him.

Clem went down stiffly and stubbornly. He twisted to look at Jess. "I can't understand Slattery at all!" he exclaimed loudly, then emphasized this with a quick headshake. "He's outnumbered, he can't win."

From the lumpy shape of a young cowboy lying close by came a response to this: "Mr. Brite, if you can convince Slattery of that, I sure wish you'd hurry up and do it."

Clem ignored this to continue squinting ahead into the yard. "What can he gain, Jess? What can he possibly hope to gain?"

Jess was watching a particular gunman down in the yard when he replied: "He's not thinking rational, Clem. He's thinking wild and acting wild."

A yonder gunman fired again and ducked back behind the blacksmith shop.

"He'll get a lot of men killed for nothin', Jess."

"When you buy gunmen, Clem, you don't care about their lives . . . only their guns." Jess snugged back his carbine, waiting for the gunman behind the blacksmith shop to jump out and fire again.

"He'll likely get killed too, though!" exclaimed old Brite. "He's not *that* crazy, is he?"

Jess remained silent and still, his carbine cocked, his trigger finger lightly curved and waiting. "He's that crazy all right," he muttered aside. Then more loudly: "He's got some idea that if he survives, and I don't survive, he'll be able to get a slice of Big B."

The gunman sprang from the shelter down by the smithy, threw up his carbine—and Jess pressed his trigger.

The gunman went drunkenly back against the shed and dropped his gun. It exploded upon striking the ground, plowing up a long dust streamer.

Clem saw this and approved. "Good shooting!" he crowed, and pushed out his own carbine seeking a target. "How many men's he got down there, you reckon?"

"I don't know, Clem. Maybe ten, maybe fifteen. I don't think he ever had more than twenty."

Clem grunted. "Haw! And we got no less than fifty."

Jess was thinking privately that Slattery's ten or fifteen were nearly a match for his fifty, as far as shooting ability went, but he said nothing.

The Big B cowboys pinned down at the main house and down in the log bunkhouse stepped up their fire, encouraged in this by the arrival of Jess's posse. Several of them even hooted derisively at Slattery's men, calling out taunts and curses.

Slattery's men did not reply to this, nor did Jess expect them too. After all, these were professional killers. They had only one interest in this battle, and that was to earn their pay by doing as much damage as they could for Mike Slattery. They could not remain impersonal—no man could in a fight that endangered his life—but they could and did refrain from anything but the deadly business at hand.

It became apparent to Jess, as he lay there with the cowmen and townsmen firing around him, that Slattery had struck Big B from approximately the same position Jess's men now held, and that they had worked their way down closer, and that if Jess hadn't arrived when he did, they probably would have overcome the defenders at the main house.

The bunkhouse held most of Big B's defenders. Furthermore, because this little building was square, massively built, and had only one door and two windows, Slattery could not hope to storm it. But he could have, in all probability, overcome resistance from the main house, for here there did not seem to be more than six guns in action. Additionally, because the house was much larger and better ventilated, six people could not be expected to adequately defend it against twice their number of approaching enemies.

Jess thought that Mike Slattery's strategy had been to gain the main house, use his mother and the others there as hostages to force capitulation of the men at the bunkhouse, and then afterward to wait in hiding for Jess himself to ride in. The reason he thought this now was because Slattery's gun crew was, in the main, already well south of the bunkhouse on its way toward the main house.

A man inched up where Jess lay and grunted down flat beside him. It was Jack Parsons. He said of Mike Slattery: "Give him a chance to give up. He don't stand a chance, and by now he ought to know it."

Before Jess could reply to this, old Clem slammed a shot down into the yonder yard, then flung his head around toward Parsons saying: "Give him nothing! Give him a bullet in the guts!"

Jess, gazing down across that moonlighted yard, watched those winking red bursts for a moment before speaking. Then, finally, he said to Parsons: "I've tried to reason with Mike before. It doesn't work."

"Not Mike!" exclaimed Parsons swiftly. "His men. They sure know how this'll end if they don't quit, Jess."

Jess nodded. He did not expect to accomplish anything, but he felt he should at least make the effort. He lay for a while, waiting for a lull in the gunfire. When it ultimately came, he yelled out into the echoing hush.

"This is Jess Bennett of Big B. Listen to me, you fellows down in the yard. There are fifty men with me out here. If you don't give up, you'll get killed. Don't let Slattery get you buried."

A ragged burst of gunfire came from the yard in the general direction of Jess's shout. He and Parsons pressed flat, and off a few feet, old Clem Brite growled muffled curses with his face in the dirt.

The cattlemen around Jess fired a furious volley down into the yard. It was a deafening fusillade, and for a moment those gunmen out there were too occupied ducking low to fire back.

In this interlude Jess tried once more, his voice coming on strong in the wake of that single volley.

"Mike, call it off! You're whipped! You'll only get a lot of men hurt by keeping this up!"

Slattery's grating bull-bass voice came back at once. "You quit, Jess!" he roared. "If you push us, we'll storm the house. I know your ma and wife-to-be are in there. If you don't quit, them women are goin' to get hurt. Get on your damned horses and ride out of here . . . all but you, Jess. I want you."

Parsons said roughly: "He wouldn't do that. He wouldn't bother the womenfolk, would he?"

"Like hell he wouldn't," snapped old Clem, rubbing dirt from his face with both fists. "He'll do it all right."

Jess, believing Clem spoke truthfully, said: "He's desperate enough, Jack. He'll do it if he can."

Jess had placed the approximate position of Slattery's voice. He was either inside the log barn or very close to it. "Keep an eye on the barn," he murmured to Clem and Parsons. "As long as Mike stays in there . . . as long as we can keep him in there . . . I don't think the others will do much more than defend themselves. He's their leader."

Clem blew dust from his carbine, bent low over it, and let off a shot in the direction of the barn. As he was levering up another bullet, others close by also fired at the barn. Gradually then, the gunfire increased again, and all of Jess's men, taking their cue from Clem and one or two others, began directing their shots against the barn. The night was filled with the thunder of carbines and six-guns. The air became redolent with the acrid smell of burned powder.

Slattery's gunmen returned their fire but not as savagely as they had before. It appeared to Jess that they were puzzled by the heavy concentration upon the barn. It must, he thought, presage something to those men down in the yard.

Actually, it was a fluke. Jess had neither ordered nor expected such a concentration of fire against the barn. He also correctly surmised that when the possemen tired of shooting this way, they would change targets. But for the time being, anyway, he was relieved of any concern about Mike Slattery trying to leave the barn.

He rolled up onto his side, reloading. Nearby, Clem Brite was lying sprawled, carbine snugged back, dirty old leathery face hunched low, firing from time to time and seeming entirely engrossed in this work.

Jess finished reloading and went down flat again.

Jack Parsons, on his right, raised his head long enough to say: "Maybe we ought to divide up and try slippin' around 'em east and west, Jess."

"It'd increase the danger," stated Jess. "This way we aren't likely to hit anyone we don't want to hit. Your way . . . we might catch Slattery in a crossfire, but in this lousy light, we'd probably hit a few of our own men, too."

Clem raised up to growl: "I'd give five hundred good cows right this minute for a cannon!" Then he dropped down and began firing again.

Jess grinned in spite of himself.

Parsons stopped shooting. He raised up with his head slightly cocked. After a while, wearing a little frown, he said: "Jess, it doesn't sound to me like there are as many men down there."

"'Course not," growled old Clem. "With all the lead we've put into the yard, some of 'em were bound to get hit."

But Parsons shook his head at this. "Maybe one or two," he conceded, "but those men are pretty savvy about keepin' down. No, it's not that. What I think happened is that some of 'em must have slipped away. Got smart and while the firin' was at its peak, just got up and slipped off in the night."

Jess, gauging the gunfire from the yard with particular attention now, decided that Parsons was correct. He had to agree that in fact there was not as much answering gunfire as there had been when they'd first come up.

He said: "I hope the ones who run out go east or south where Coulter's posse will hear them."

Now, the possemen were rerouting their gunfire. No longer were the barn's defenders unable to fire back because of the ferocity of that concentrated shooting. This brought Jess's attention to the men in the barn again. He got down behind his carbine, waiting for someone to run out down there. Time passed though, and no one emerged.

There was a rear doorway to the barn, but it led over open country all the way to the creek. Jess figured that no man in his right mind would attempt getting clear this way. The clouds shifted and moonlight hit that open ground bringing it to a brightness that had no counterpart anywhere else.

If Slattery tried leaving the barn this way, he would be a long way from his gun crew, and before he could run along the barn's south side returning to the yard, he would have to pass along the full length of the nearby bunkhouse's north wall. This, Jess was confident, would be even more fatal to him than that moonlit area behind the barn would be.

But—and Jess was convinced of this—Slattery had to do something. He was losing men, from whatever cause, by remaining static. He would know this even better than Jess would. He was down in the yard, much closer to his own crew. That diminishing return fire would attract his attention, too.

Jess leaned far over toward Parsons. "Watch the barn," he directed. "Slattery is in there, I'm sure. But he'll have to try and leave pretty quick now."

Parsons muttered his agreement to this. Jess then leaned far over in the opposite direction and repeated this order to Clem Brite. He got another brusque head wag, and Clem shifted his position slightly upon the ground so that he could adequately cover the barn area from where he lay.

Farther along, on both sides of these three, for a hundred yards, Jess's men were still firing at muzzle blasts.

Down in the yard, Slattery's gunfighters were beginning to change their positions. It appeared to Jess they did this in order to get better cover and also to shorten the line which they began to understand was thinning out around them.

Suddenly, a number of running horses burst out of the yard, driven northward towards Jess's line by Slattery's men. These animals, terrified by the gunshots behind them, raced furiously and blindly onward.

Jess raised a shout to alert his men. At once other voices took up this cry. Men rolled frantically to get clear. Others sprang up and went running out of the pathway of those maddened animals. Jess and those nearest him were not in direct line of that flinging charge. They concentrated on firing down into the yard to discourage whatever Slattery's men were up to. But this necessitated changing their direction and leaving the barn unwatched for a brief time.

It dawned on Jess, after those stampeded horses had passed clear of his men on the north, what the purpose of that stampede had been. He fired into the barn to draw fire—and drew none. He swore with feeling. Mike Slattery and those gunmen who had been with him in the barn had made good their escape during the diversion.

Now Jess was once more chilled by that same premonition that had warned him twice earlier of great peril. He tried to locate men down in the yard and failed. Also, that fierce gunfire had lessened considerably, which meant only one thing now.

Slattery was gathering his men. He had something new in mind.

CHAPTER SIXTEEN

The firing from the north beyond Big B's yard began to dwindle when no return shots came upward from Slattery's gunmen. Gradually, men's rising voices could be heard along the posse's line, and old Clem Brite raised up a tired and puckered face. Like the others, Clem put his rummaging gaze down into the yard. His brows rolled together perplexedly at this growing stillness.

On Jess's other side, Jack Parsons also rose up to squint ahead. "What the hell?" he muttered, more to himself than to those around him.

Jess put aside his carbine. He looked out where Big B's bunkhouse lay in solid gloom. There was no sound coming from there, either. And on ahead, at the main house, this new stillness also lay.

A man far down the line on Jess's right said: "I don't like this." The man's words carried easily in the quiet.

Jess got up to one knee. No shot came. He stood upright and

still no shot came. Clem Brite, twisting to look up, began to arise as well.

Jess said: "Stay down."

Clem grimaced, and he made no further attempt to rise up.

"They ain't ridin' off," someone mumbled, down the line from Clem. "Else we'd hear their horses."

"No," Jess stated thoughtfully. "Slattery won't give up like that." As he spoke he started moving forward.

Jack Parsons called quickly to him: "Hey, don't go down there! That's probably what they're waitin' for . . . some of us to make good targets."

But Jess had another reason in mind for this sudden hush. He kept on walking. He got within a hundred yards of the barn and halted there where a cottonwood tree stood. The yard ahead was as still as death. Faintly, there came a rustling sound from within the bunkhouse. Jess could imagine those troubled men in there squirming upright for a look out into the yard.

After so much gunfire, this silence was almost as deafening as the thundering of the guns had been.

He stood by the tree blocking in squares of the yard, examining each of these for the shape or shadow of a man. He found no sign of Slattery or his gun crew at all.

Farther along, where the main house stood, all was darkness, all was stillness. That, he told himself, would be Slattery's objective now—the main house. He thought of his mother in there, of Margaret Lawton who he was to marry shortly. And finally of little Linda Louise, Dr. Jacob Hartman, and the two or three Big B ranch hands who were also in there—or at least who he felt certain were in there, because he had counted six distinct gun flashes coming from the house at the height of that earlier fighting.

He shook away that premonition and closed his thoughts

around what he must do now. He did not know yet whether Slattery's embattled men were inside the house. He was only certain that this would be their goal because they had to secure cover, and fast. And, thinking as Slattery undoubtedly now also thought, he felt the gunmen would want hostages.

He walked away from the cottonwood tree, angled down behind the log barn, and took a deep breath before sprinting rapidly over that moonlighted bare place, and got to the barn's south wall. Ahead of him now was the bunkhouse. He stopped dead still, knowing full well that unless he identified himself before moving again, he would be shot by his own cowboys in the blurred night. He did not, however, wish to call out, to identify himself in a manner that would alert the gunmen.

He pondered his choices—darting over to the bunkhouse and getting along its north wall so that the men inside could not angle their weapons downward toward him, or simply walking over, hands high, until he could safely identify himself without shouting.

He decided upon the latter course, perilous as it was for the elemental reason that if he ran and was fired upon, Slattery, with his own men around him, would know instantly that someone was infiltrating from the north. He pushed away from the barn, hoisted both arms rigidly overhead, and began walking.

Moonlight striking the carbine barrel in his right hand was instantly seen by someone at the bunkhouse window. A man's voice snapped a warning inside. Jess heard a gun grate over wood. He heard the cocking mechanism function, and his stomach knotted at this little, quick sound. But he kept on walking, keeping his stare steadily upon that aimed and unmoving gun, scarcely daring to breathe.

A hoarsely toned but dead calm voice said: "You there . . . you tryin' to surrender?"

Jess walked on. He still was too far out to answer aloud, so he simply nodded his head vigorously and continued to pace along.

"Then drop that damned carbine," said that lethally soft voice.

Jess went the final ten feet and halted. He looked upward, trying to recognize the man curled about that carbine.

"It's Jess Bennett," he said in a low voice. "I didn't dare call out who I was before."

The face behind that carbine came flinging up and was recognizable as John Burr, without his hat. He blinked outward and downward, before he said: "Tilt your head back."

Jess obeyed.

Burr let off a shaky breath. "Damn," he whispered. "I don't think you'll ever know how close you just come to gettin' killed, Jess." Burr drew in a whistling big breath and turned around to say: "One of you boys, go and open the front door a crack. It's Jess."

Jess lowered his arms, went to the corner of the bunkhouse, and paused there to run a carefully searching look roundabout. The stillness was holding. He swung over into plain sight, gained the bunkhouse porch where dripping darkness at once hid him, and moved on inside.

At once Big B riders pushed up close. It was very dark in that bunkhouse. Jess saw faces only as oily white blurs until his eyes ultimately became accustomed to the gloom.

John Burr pushed his way forward, saying: "Where are the men you brought with you?"

"Still back out there," answered Jess quickly. "What's bothering me is where Slattery and his hired guns are."

"Gone," said a cowboy in a voice charged with powerful conviction. "Got a bellyful of fightin' and rode away."

Jess shook his head. "Did you hear them ride away?" he

challenged them. When no one answered this, he said: "They're still here. Mike Slattery isn't giving up that easy."

Burr pursed his lips. He said: "Well . . .?"

"At the house," stated Jess.

"Naw," a rider scoffed. "Three o' our boys are in there along with Miss Margaret and your ma, Jess. They couldn't have got in there 'thout a scrap, and we'd have heard it."

John Burr put a dark look upon this man. He then returned his speculative look to Jess. "Let's get out of here and find out," he said. "Between us and the men you got, it won't matter where Slattery's hired guns are . . . we'll make mincemeat out of 'em."

From back in a dark corner now came a new voice. It was Slim Perkins who had been wounded during Slattery's earlier attack on Big B.

Perkins said dryly to Burr: "John, you aren't usin' your head. I'm livin' proof . . . but just barely . . . that them fellers are topnotch gunslingers. You go bustin' up toward the house and it'll be *you* that comes out mincemeat. An' as for gettin' in up there . . . well, don't fool yourself. One man in his stockin' feet could slip in through a window and put a gun on them folks until his friends got inside, too."

This was, as it eventually turned out, exactly what had happened. But at that moment, neither Jess nor any of the others could be certain of this. Not until a solitary gunshot from the main house broke off their talk and took them over toward the door and windows.

Then came the unmistakable voice of Mike Slattery, loudly charged with triumph. "Hey, Jess! I know you're out there somewhere. You listen to me, Mr. Big B. Me an' my boys got your ma and Margaret Lawton, that little girl, Doc Hartman, and three of your stupid riders under our guns in here."

Slattery paused for a long while, obviously to let those who heard him consider what he was saying. Then he laughed, and that sound, even more than his words, struck down icily into Jess, and called out again.

"If you want, charge the house. I'd like for you idiots out there to try that. First, I'll knock off Doc Hartman. Then your three cowboys . . . one at a time. And after them . . . you guess, Jess, who'll get it next."

A rawboned big and wasted hand came forth from the bunkhouse darkness to brush over Jess's arm.

It was Samuel Patton. He said softly: "Billy Ray is in there, too. He was seeing Linda Louise when they struck."

Until Patton had spoken, Jess had not recognized Samuel in the darkness; had not, in fact, even remembered him over the course of the events of this long and perilous night. Now it struck him that Slattery had not mentioned having Billy Ray a prisoner, too, and while he instantly decided Slattery had perhaps overlooked the lad because he was not, right then, important, the omission nevertheless stuck in Jess's mind.

"Hey Jess! You tongue-tied? Why don't you speak up?" shouted Slattery. "You too worried now? Well, if you are . . . that's fine, because all I want for you is to listen to what I'm goin' to tell you." There was another pause, then, sounding angry now, Slattery yelled harshly: "Jess, damn you, can you hear me?"

"I can hear you!" called back Jess. "Say what you're going to, Slattery."

Slattery's booming voice softened again, losing its flash of temper and sounding triumphant. "Sure, I'll say what I'm goin' to say. And you'll damned well listen, too."

Slattery started to say something else, but an indistinguishable, hard, and bleak voice interrupted him. Jess could make out only one sentence when this unfamiliar voice opened up. "Get on with it, damn it, Slattery." There was more, and a fiery swift exchange here, but finally only Slattery's voice persisted, coming on loud again.

"Jess, we're comin' out of here, and we'll have your ma and your sweetheart with us. We'll also have old Hartman and your three riders . . . oh, and the little girl. They'll be our guarantee that won't any of those damned fools with you fire on us."

Samuel Patton's fingers brushed Jess's sleeve again. He shouldered past John Burr to say quickly: "Don't let them move Linda Louise. Please don't let them do that."

Jess put a hard glance upon Samuel, saw the frantic expression of appeal, and nodded before facing forward again, toward the distant, dark, and bullet-scarred house.

"You hear that, Jess?"

"I heard you, Mike. And I've got one thing to say to you."

"Say it!"

"Don't move the little girl. Leave her in her bed. Rough handling might kill her."

"It sure might," crowed Slattery. "Doc just said the same thing."

"Then leave her out of this."

"Haw!" boomed Slattery. "Next thing you'll ask is for us to leave your ma behind . . . and then Margaret Lawton, too."

"Don't touch the little girl, Slattery."

"No? An' what'll you do if we drag her out with us?"

"Kill you," Jess responded in a very even, very steady voice. "Kill you . . . even if it kills me to do it."

Again, there came that deep and bitter voice from within the house, saying something to Slattery. This time Slattery's response was wrathful and strong. He called that unidentified man a name. Jess and the listening others could only speculate, but it sounded from within the house as though a fight had only barely been averted by others. For a while after this, there was no more shouting from the house. During this interval Jess turned to John Burr.

"Get out of here, and head north to where my posse is," he ordered. "Bring them back down here, John, on their doggoned tiptoes if necessary, but they're not to make a sound. Fetch them around behind the barn where they can't be seen from the house. Remember, John . . . *not a single sound!*"

Burr shuffled along the bunkhouse front wall, stepped off the porch, sprinted quietly toward the rear of the barn, and then in a northward direction.

"Hey, Jess! We'll leave the kid. You hear me, Jess?"

"How can I help it," Jess answered testily. "They can probably hear you all the way to Hereford. So all right, you're going to leave the little girl."

"Now you listen close!" roared Slattery, ignoring Jess's remark about his shouting. "And you listen good. We're comin' out of here with our hostages. We're goin' along the front of your house and then out of here to the west where our horses are. Then we're goin' to ride out of here . . . *with our hostages!*"

Jess's heart sank. Around him the Big B men let off a collective soft sigh.

"We'll turn 'em all loose," continued Slattery, "when we're plumb away from here . . . and safe. You understand now what's going to be, Jess?"

"I understand."

"Now, there's one more thing. You, Jess. I want you to walk out into the center of the yard where I can see you when we come out." Slattery's voice turned sly, turned crafty. "That's so I'll know where you are . . . and know that you and the others aren't up to anything."

Close to Jess's ear, Samuel Patton said: "No, don't agree to that. He only wants to know where you are so he can shoot you."

The others around Jess at the bunkhouse doorway voiced strong assent to this.

"Jess, damn you . . . do you hear me?" Slattery yelled. "Did you hear what I just said?"

"I heard you," replied Jess. Then he added: "Don't come out yet, Mike. I've got to get word to all my men that this is a truce. Otherwise, they'll open up as soon as you leave the house."

"So hurry and get it done!" called Slattery. "Make it fast."

CHAPTER SEVENTEEN

Jess turned to the men with him at the bunkhouse. He said: "We won't stop Slattery's crew from riding out of here . . . but they've got to do it alone." He did not explain about Les Coulter and the men waiting on the plain south and west of the Big B. He did not think he had time for such an explanation, and he did not, in fact, because John Burr now returned at the head of that big force from the north beyond the yard. Leading these men behind Burr was hobbling Clem Brite and lanky Jack Parsons.

Jess took his Big B riders from the bunkhouse, told Burr to take them on foot northward out of sight and sound, then downcountry to the south so that they would be in position to attack Slattery if and when Jess shouted them the order.

He then had Jack Parsons take some of the larger party of armed men westward beyond the yard, explaining to Clem and Parsons his reasons for this.

"There'll be trouble. I'm sure of that, and when Slattery's men break up, some of them may try to run, head west. Jack, you'll be out there to stop them."

"With bullets?" Parsons queried.

"With bullets," stated Jess, and added to this: "Be quiet though."

Clem Brite poked his head around the bunkhouse for a long look at the main house. "Sure quiet," he said, drawing back again. "You sure they ain't already left?"

Jess was sure. He looked at the men Parsons was leading off, then tried in that dim light to count the men left with him, including old Clem. Thirteen or fourteen. He beckoned these men forward to the bunkhouse wall and halted them there. Samuel Patton was beside him, breathing with difficulty. He wore no gun around his middle and carried no carbine.

"Hey, Mike!" Jess called loudly, and almost at once got back his flat answer.

"Yeah? You got them fellers warned what'll happen if they fire when we come outside? Because if you haven't, you know what's goin' to happen to your ma and your sweetheart."

Jess made no reply to this.

"I'll make sure none of my men are near your horses, otherwise some of your hotheads may start shooting, and if that happens, Mike, not a one of you will live through it . . . or your hostages, either."

Slattery was briefly silent, then he said: "You know the horses are back of the house here with a couple of my boys. So warn your men to keep away from there. Now you ready for us to come out, Jess?"

Jess then went swiftly over his plan before replying. He did not see how Slattery and his gun crew could possibly escape—unless they were able to keep their hostages. In that case, Jess knew, none of his cowmen or townsmen would fire upon them, and they would indeed get clear.

"You better answer up," yelled Slattery, "an' you'd better be ready, 'cause we're tired of waitin'."

"Mike, you've got to let the hostages go before you ride off."

Slattery's profanity was loud and shocking. "I'm dictatin' the terms here," he roared, "not you. I say we take them with us."

"Then," replied Jess, "my men refuse to hold their fire when you come out."

"Are you crazy?" demanded Slattery. "They'll get killed!"

"So will you, Slattery. So will every man jack with you. I give you my word on that. There are fifty men out here who have sworn to shoot every damned one of you . . . to give you no quarter at all . . . unless you agree to let the hostages go as soon as you're mounted up."

Slattery swore again, he ranted and bellowed, until, within the house, others quieted him. Jess and the men along the bunkhouse wall at his side plainly heard the fierce argument in progress within the house. Finally, a voice none of them recognized called out.

"Bennett? How do we know you'll let us ride out of here if we let the prisoners go?"

Jess had his reply ready for this. "We'll walk out where you can see us and throw down our guns. Will that satisfy you?"

There was another heated discussion in the house, then that same rough voice said: "All right, toss down your guns. Throw them out into the yard."

"And you'll swear to release the hostages?"

"Yes."

Jess turned. Clem Brite had a sour and dissenting expression on his face, but he was the first man to go stiffly forward, drop his weapons, and walk back behind the bunkhouse. Other men also started forward. As fast as these men came back out of sight of the main house, Jess grabbed them, pointed toward the barn, and said: "Go get pitchforks, spades, harness hames, anything that in this darkness can count as a gun, and walk out to toss these things on that pile of guns."

"Huh?" grunted Clem. "What for, Jess?"

"Because, dammit, those men will be counting you. They're too far off to recognize any of you, or even be sure what you're throwing down, but they'll be counting you to be certain all the possemen are here with me." Jess gave Clem and several others rough shoves toward the barn.

Men continued to walk forth into the yard, adding to that heap of weapons. After a time, other men also strode solemnly forth to toss down objects which were not weapons at all, but which clattered down upon the heap of guns anyway. Jess kept close tally. When he had an approximate figure to the number of possemen who had come to the ranch with him, he threw up an arm to halt those who were ready to go on with this ruse.

When no more men walked out into sight, that rough voice called from the house: "Bennett, Slattery wants you to come over here."

Jess had been waiting for this. He still had both his own weapons, his six-gun and his Winchester saddle gun. He had not gone forth with the others in anticipation of this.

Now he said to Clem: "Stay here. Don't do a thing unless I call out for you to. You understand?"

Clem stepped in close to remonstrate. Samuel Patton shouldered Clem aside and said: "He aims to shoot you. You know that."

Jess nodded. "I know it. What else can I do?"

Patton turned suddenly silent and thoughtful. He fixed his haggard face forward. "Tell them at least to let the hostages walk out here first."

Jess nodded at this. He looked into those other dirty, tense, and oily faces. Then, to Clem Brite he said: "He might not hit me. That's what I'm gambling on. As soon as I walk out there and see movement at the house, I figure to drop. If my timing is right, I may beat the bullet."

Clem considered this carefully and very slowly began to wag his head. "It won't work, Jess. There's only one chance out of a thousand you'll be able to guess when he's going to pull the trigger."

"But there's that one chance, and I've got to take it. Listen, Clem, they won't put up with much more delay. It's a standoff, but they've got a little edge."

Samuel Patton, gazing fixedly upon Jess now with a peculiarly crafty expression, repeated his earlier words. "Tell them to turn the prisoners loose now. We've kept our end of the bargain."

Jess nodded and faced fully around to call out. Samuel moved up closer to him.

"You in there!" yelled Jess. "Keep your word. Send those people outside."

It was not the stranger who replied now, it was Mike Slattery again. He sounded fiercely bitter and deadly when he said: "They're goin' out the back way right now, Jess, with my men. They'll be turned loose." Slattery paused. There were some sharp words exchanged between him and another man inside the house.

These were the last words spoken by anyone that Jess heard for a long time. Behind him, Samuel Patton brought a big bony fist overhand and sledged it mightily into the back of Jess's neck. The struck man went down like a felled tree, rolled loosely off the bunkhouse wall, and settled in churned dirt.

Clem Brite gave a gasp. Others, held speechless for a second, only stared. In that dead moment of complete stillness Samuel said to Clem: "Help me change clothes with him. Don't ask questions, just do as I say."

Samuel bent to tear at Jess's coat, at his hat and gun belt. He rasped out at those stunned men: "Hurry! Give me a hand here. Don't just stand there!"

Clem Brite's face suddenly turned murderous. He stepped menacingly forward, both fists balled. "What the hell . . .?" he snarled.

Samuel whipped momentarily up to his full height. He stared at him. "There's no time now, Clem. You'll get your explanation later. Now . . . do as I ask . . . help me change clothes with him. I'm going to take his place in the darkness for Slattery."

Clem's fists loosened. He stared and blinked, then he also bent over Jess's unconscious form. He worked swiftly, muttering half loud, half soft, all the time he worked. "It better be real good . . . what you got in mind, mister . . . Why you willing to do this? Who are you anyway? Listen, Slattery'll kill you. He'll gun you down the second you step out into that yard. Why you doing this . . .?"

Samuel had Jess's coat. He flung down his own coat and shrugged into the younger man's garment. He was working with great haste. He buckled on Jess's shell belt and holstered pistol. Around him the silent possemen, understanding what he had in mind, still stood dumbfounded.

Finally, Samuel took Jess's hat, crushed it down upon his head, and stood up to his full, wasted height. While he looked down gravely at Jess, he said to Clem: "You explain to him, please. You tell him this was my part of the fight. Say to him . . ." Samuel stopped speaking. He shrugged his shoulders and resettled Jess's hat on his head. "Never mind," he murmured. "He'll understand."

Then Samuel pushed past Clem and strode out into the moon-lighted yard, halted, spread his legs, and faced fully toward the house. He had Jess's coat brushed clear of the sagging gun at his side. He seemed, in this brief and unforgettable moment, to be an entirely different man, a complete stranger. He had the stance, the expression, and even the shoulder-down readiness of a gunfighter.

At the bunkhouse wall, Jess stirred feebly upon the ground and moaned. Around him those rigid possemen neither heard nor heeded. They were held motionless by that onward softly lighted figure.

"Come out!" Samuel called to Mike Slattery. "Come out and fight like a man . . . unless you're too damned yellow for that!"

A shot broke the hush. Red-orange light blossomed from the house. The far door shuddered inward, and Slattery sprang clear, getting off his second shot. Samuel did not seem to have been struck at all. His right hand swooped, dipped low, and came up firing. Slattery gave a cry from deep in his throat. He got off a third shot. Samuel fired once more. Then he began to wilt, and across the yard Slattery slid gradually down off the verandah onto the hard ground, tipped over onto his face, and lay flatly still.

Samuel went down onto his knees. He gently placed Jess's gun in the dust and put forth a supporting hand to keep himself upright a little longer.

Clem Brite came abruptly to life. "It's the women," he croaked. "Yonder . . . coming around the side of the house."

Instantly, the possemen broke out into loud talking. They did not hear that furious beat of running horses as Slattery's crew fled west, as fast and as far as they could from the Big B.

"Hey," a voice said weakly from the ground at Clem's feet. "Hey . . . what the hell happened . . .?"

A number of hands reached to help Jess upright, and once he was on his feet, they supported him until he stopped weaving and could lean upon the bunkhouse wall.

Clem Brite was speaking again, turning his assessing gaze away from Jess. "Some of you go get that fellow who took Jess's place and put him on a bunk in the bunkhouse. You others . . . you go fetch the womenfolk over here."

Clem himself remained with Jess. He got a hatful of water from the trough and poured it over Jess's head, not attempting to be careful, drenching him. When Jess was loudly sputtering from

this, Clem moved his face up close, saying: "Who was that bony
big fellow who took your place out in the yard, Jess? I'll tell you
one thing . . . whatever he is now, once in his lifetime, he was
doggoned good with a pistol."

Jess gathered his wits slowly. For a while Clem's words made
no sense at all. Then, suddenly, they did. Jess pushed clear of the
wall. He looked, with widening eyes and paling cheeks, out where
some cowmen were carrying Samuel along toward the bunkhouse.
He groaned aloud.

"Why did you let him do it, Clem? Why didn't you . . .?"

"Jess! Listen here, Jess! He knocked you senseless before I knew
what was happening. Then he commenced changing clothes with
you, and I thought . . . I thought . . ."

Jess stopped listening and walked away. He went past his
mother, Margaret Lawton, and the released Big B riders as though
they did not exist at all. He went up into the bunkhouse and stood
off while Samuel was very gently put upon a bed. Then he said to
those men: "Go outside. Send Miss Margaret in here and don't let
anyone else come in here. Go on."

For a time there was only an endless silence in that bunkhouse.
Samuel lay, his eyes closed, his lips paling, and his breathing low
and labored.

When Margaret entered, she passed over to where Jess sat upon
the edge of Samuel's bunk and put forth a hand, let it lightly rest
upon his shoulder.

He looked up at her. She seemed very tired. Her lips were slack
and shadows were beneath her eyes. But she smiled at Jess, then
looked beyond, at Samuel, and her smile dwindled.

A long way off, vague now in the breaking dawn, came muffled,
ragged gunshots. Jess heard men in the yard calling quickly to
one another about this. He heard them getting on to horses, still
crying out that Coulter's men had stopped those fleeing gunmen

Slattery had imported. Then, all in a thunderous rush, the horse-men broke out of Big B's yard, and after a while that silence came closing down again.

Jess put out a hand to touch Samuel. Red stickiness darkened his fingers. He said gently: "Samuel . . . can you hear me all right?"

"Yes, Jess."

"Do you want to see Billy Ray and Linda Louise?"

Samuel was a long time answering. His head rolled feebly. "No. It would be better this way." He made a good effort to focus his opened eyes upon Jess, upon Margaret standing behind Jess. "Jess? There's something I've got to ask . . . you."

Jess quietly wagged his head. "I know," he murmured. "Don't fret about it, Samuel. I talked to Margaret about it the other night over at her folks' place. She knows . . . she wants to keep them both. We'll do for them, Samuel. We'll raise them like our own. You have my word on that."

A smile settled across Samuel's lips. This moment, all the worry, all the struggle and hardship and loneliness left his face. He moved his head again, weaker this time. A little low sigh passed his lips, and he settled flatter upon the bunk.

Jess rose up and turned, taking Margaret's arm. On another bunk, large-eyed and still, lay Slim Perkins. He watched them go out of the bunkhouse and gently close the door.

Jess let go of Margaret's hand. His attention was caught by a familiar, piping young voice. He swung toward the main house. Clem Brite, as filthy as a man could be, and hobbling with a more pronounced limp now, was crossing forward from the verandah with Billy Ray clinging to his fingers.

Jess said to Margaret, without taking his eyes from old Clem and young Billy Ray: "Do you know why he did it that way?"

Margaret answered quietly: "I think so, yes. It was his way of cheating that other death. His way of dying for a good cause and as a brave man. Something for his son and daughter to remember and cherish."

Jess turned. His look was wondering. It plainly said he had not anticipated this kind of comprehension.

Margaret took his hand and led him across the yard. There, she released him saying: "You tell him, Jess. I'll go in with Linda Louise."

As Billy Ray and Clem came up and halted by Jess, Margaret looked at Clem. "Come help me make some coffee," she said, and walked off with Clem, leaving Jess and Billy Ray standing there looking gravely at one another.

"I was with Linda Louise when they came this time," the boy said. "I got under her bed, and they didn't find me." He put his hand into Jess's. "I was going to fight them if they tried to do anything to her."

Jess nodded, then said: "I've got something to tell you, son. There's no easy way to do it, but let's walk down by the creek. It's private down there if a fellow feels like crying. When I was your age, before my pa died, I used to go there often. The day he died . . . I stayed down there all day in the tree shade, just listening to the creek. It made me feel a lot better."

Dawn came while they were slowly pacing past the battered bunkhouse, around the big log barn. Its first fresh light held that same eternal promise Samuel had seen in it, for Samuel's son and for the man who would now be the father to Samuel's son.

THE END

ABOUT THE AUTHOR

Lauran Paine, under his own name and various pseudonyms, has written over a thousand books. He was born in Duluth, Minnesota. His family moved to California when he was at a young age, and his apprenticeship as a Western writer came about through the years he spent in the livestock trade, rodeos, and even motion pictures, where he served as an extra because of his expert horsemanship in several films starring movie cowboy Johnny Mack Brown. In the late 1930s, Paine trapped wild horses in northern Arizona and even, for a time, worked as a professional farrier. Paine came to know the Old West through the eyes of many who had been born in the nineteenth Century, and he learned that Western life had been very different from the way it was portrayed on the screen. "I knew men who had killed other men," he later recalled. "But they were the exceptions. Prior to and during the Depression, people were just too busy eking out an existence to indulge in Saturday-night brawls." He served in the US Navy in the Second World War and began writing for Western pulp magazines following his discharge. It is interesting to note that his earliest novels (written under his own name and the pseudonym Mark Carrel) were published in the British market, and he soon had as strong a following in that country as in the United States. Paine's Western fiction is characterized by strong plots, authenticity, an apparently effortless ability to construct situation and character, and a preference for building his stories upon a solid foundation of historical fact. *Adobe Empire* (1956), one of his best novels, is a fictionalized account of the last twenty years in the life of trader William Bent and, in an off-trail way, has a melancholy, bittersweet texture that is not easily forgotten. In later novels like *The White Bird* (1997) and *Cache Cañon* (1998), he showed that the special magic and power of his stories and characters had only matured along with his basic themes of changing times, changing attitudes, learning from experience, respecting nature, and the yearning for a simpler, more moderate way of life.